Naughty Santa

JANELLE DENISON

Prologue

*G*o ahead. *Do it. No one will* *ever find out.*
This gleeful goad came from the little devil sitting on Amanda Creighton's left shoulder. Of course Devilish Desiree—the name Amanda had given the more daring part of her conscience—was a figment of her own imagination. Still, the little female devil always seemed to pop up whenever the tiniest glimmer of a naughty thought happened to cross Amanda's mind. With her red sparkly halter top, short miniskirt and matching four-inch heels, Desiree was ready and willing to lead Amanda straight into all sorts of temptation.

Thank God she had Angelic Angie, the prim and proper angel who sat on her right shoulder, to counter Desiree's wicked suggestions. Even now, Angie was fighting to preserve Amanda's integrity.

Don't do it, Amanda, Angie said in that reproachful tone she normally used when Desiree was involved. *You know it's wrong.*

Desiree rolled her eyes and crossed one long red silk-stocking leg over the other. *Don't listen to her,* she whispered in Amanda's ear. *She's such a Goody Two-Shoes, and that halo above her head is just way too straight and shiny, if you ask me. She's the reason why you never have any fun.*

Amanda leaned back in her office chair and rubbed her temples with the pads of her fingers. She found it hard to argue Desiree's point because when it came to any indecision Amanda might have about right or wrong, or the merest thought about doing something mischievous, Angie's logic and rationale always won out. And that meant Amanda usually did the *honorable* thing, which made her way too uptight and boring, in Desiree's estimation.

It had been that way since Amanda was twelve. Desiree and Angie had arrived shortly after her mother had died, and they'd been with her ever since, playing tug-of-war with her psyche. After the loss of her mother, and as the only child of her workaholic father, she'd spent a lot of time alone, trying to make decisions for herself—which was what had undoubtedly prompted Desiree and Angie's initial appearance. As a young girl, they'd kept her from making bad choices, or succumbing to peer pressure at school.

Even now that Amanda was twenty-seven, they both still believed that they each knew what was best for her and had no qualms about stating their opinions on various matters—from family issues, to the clothes she bought—even the men she chose to date.

Today, it had been a brief "what if" scenario with the office's bad boy, Christian Miller—whom she had a major crush on—that had prompted a visit from Desiree. The impish she-devil had been enthusiastic about encouraging the inappropriate ideas dancing in Amanda's mind, which was quickly followed by Angie and her attempts at damage control.

With a shake of her head, Amanda picked up the neat, handwritten list of names she'd been reviewing before being interrupted by the voices of her conscience. When she'd volunteered to organize this year's Secret Santa list for the executive floor's holiday party, she'd figured it would be a relatively easy and simple task.

Connoisseur, a food and travel magazine that was owned by her father, was a large publishing company that was made up of many different departments and levels—each of which were having their holiday parties on whatever day suited their group the best. The executive floor, which also included accounting, human resources and sales, had taken a vote, and the Friday before Christmas had won out for their get-together and Secret Santa exchange.

As executive editor of *Connoisseur,* and her father's

right-hand woman, Amanda had developed a reputation for being well-organized, efficient and dependable, so everyone seemed perfectly happy when she'd offered to be the keeper of the list.

For the most part, coordinating the Secret Santa gift exchange had been just a matter of putting all of the office employees' names into a paper bag, then letting each person draw a piece of paper to find out who they'd be purchasing a gift for. Amanda kept a master list of who picked whom, and went ahead and randomly drew names for the employees who were out for the day. Everything had been going smoothly, until she'd opened the piece of paper she'd picked for Stacey Roberts, the office bimbo, and had read the name *Christian Miller,* the top sales executive for the magazine.

Amanda's pulse had raced, as it always did when it came to Christian. With his pitch-black hair, dark blue eyes and a body made for sin, he was the stuff that made up most of her deepest, fondest fantasies. Adding to his good looks was a charming, flirtatious personality and a smile that had the ability to melt polar ice caps. It was no wonder most of the women in the office had a secret crush on him. Herself included.

As much as she knew that Stacey would love to be paired up with Christian—preferably horizontally if the busty blonde had her way—Amanda couldn't bring herself to give Stacey that kind of satisfaction, which the other woman would undoubtedly exploit to her advantage.

That was when Amanda's thoughts had drifted and she'd fantasized about keeping Christian for herself, and giving Stacey her office archrival slut, Melissa Wintz, instead. The thought of pairing up those two she-cats held a whole lot of appeal and would no doubt add some fun to the gift exchange.

Come on, Amanda, Desiree cajoled. *You know you want to switch those names so you can be Christian's Secret Santa. And why not? You've been attracted to him for the past year. Besides, he's gorgeous, single and hotter than Hades.*

Amanda grinned at Desiree's amusing play on words, until Angie jumped in with her side of things.

He's all wrong for you, she said with a disapproving shake of her head. *He doesn't do relationships and he has a reputation for being a player. Don't you remember when he got caught in the boardroom in a very compromising position with that hussy from production?*

Amanda remembered the scandalous incident very well, which had caused a flurry of office speculation and gossip to run rampant about Christian's sexual prowess. Those juicy, titillating rumors had served to add plenty of spice to the personal fantasies *she'd* had about the man, and also made her wish she had the nerve to be as bold and brazen as the woman he'd been with.

Unfortunately, she also recalled her father's disappointment when he'd summoned the pair into his office the very next day to deliver a reprimand, along with a warning to keep their hands, and other body parts, to themselves during work hours. Luckily for Christian, the issue had become a moot point when the production assistant had quit two weeks later.

He's a ladies' man and a philanderer, Angie went on with determination. *He has more notches on his bedpost than you have designer shoes in your closet.*

Gorgeous stilettos that rarely see the light of day, I might add, Desiree said as she admired her own red heels that did amazing things for her legs. *It's a crime not to wear all those amazing shoes you buy.*

Leave it to Angie to use her one guilty pleasure to press her point home, and Desiree to mourn the fact that Amanda's huge shoe collection went unappreciated. Amanda definitely had a weakness for sexy shoes, with Jimmy Choo and Manolo Blahnik topping as her favorite designers. They were all openly displayed in her walk-in closet for her to look at, touch and even slip on her feet occasionally.

But Desiree was right—she didn't wear them outside of her house. Four-inch heels weren't practical for everyday wear, and those fun, sexy shoes didn't exactly go with the business suits and modest outfits she wore at the office. At least not without attracting a whole lot of attention, including her father's scrutiny. Amanda had long ago decided that as some women collected porcelain dolls or rare figurines that they displayed for their viewing pleasure, she did the same with designer shoes.

Your shoe fetish aside, being a womanizer isn't necessarily a bad thing, Desiree stated, bringing the conversation back to Christian and all the reasons why Amanda ought to consider having a fling with him. *And so what if he doesn't do relationships? What more could a girl want for Christmas than a holiday dalliance with someone who is built like a God and knows what he's doing in the sack?*

Amanda winced at that last remark. Desiree was obviously referring to her last steady boyfriend, whom she'd referred to as the one-minute wonder because of his lack of stamina when it came down to doing the deed. Once in, once out, and he was done for the night, leaving Amanda to her own devices if she wanted an orgasm.

But it hadn't been just the bad sex that had brought their relationship to an end. Like most of the men who wanted to date Amanda, he'd been more attracted to her name, wealth, and what her very powerful publisher-father could do for him and his own career.

Lips pursed, Angie smoothed a hand down her immaculate white gown. *Christian is all wrong for you, and after that fiasco in the boardroom, your father would hardly approve of him as a suitor.*

Suitor? It's not like she's going to marry the guy. Besides, Daddy wouldn't ever have to find out that she's getting some on the side from the office stud. A sly grin curved the corners of Desiree's lips. *Don't forget, he's been quite respectable the past eight months or so. He's cleaned up his act and been quite focused lately.*

Only because there's a promotion on the line, Angie argued pointedly. *He has his eye on that promotion to sales director. He wants to impress Amanda's father by proving that he's a responsible, reliable team player now instead of the cad he was back in the boardroom.*

True, Desiree agreed as she glanced at her fire-engine red painted fingernails. *But he can't remain a monk forever, and that could certainly work to Amanda's advantage.*

The banter in her head was making Amanda crazy. "Arghhh! Stop already," she ordered the two of them in a firm tone, grateful that her office door was closed so no one could hear this bizarre conversation she seemed to be having with herself. "I never said I wanted to have an affair with him."

Desiree leaned close and whispered in her ear. *You might not have said it out loud, but you've thought about it plenty. I would know since I spend a lot of time in that head of yours.*

Way too much time, Amanda was beginning to realize. And when had this discussion gotten so out of hand? She'd only pondered the idea of switching names to be Christian's Secret Santa—*secret* being the operative word—and it had blown into a full-fledged attack on her lack of a love life.

Amanda inhaled a deep, calming breath. "I'm *not* going to have a fling with him."

The halo above Angie's head shone brightly as she cast the red devil on Amanda's shoulder a triumphant smile. *Good girl.*

Desiree shook her head in disappointment. *You're going to die without ever experiencing true passion and mind-blowing sex.*

Amanda couldn't take it anymore. "Go away, both of you," she muttered.

But...

"Go. *Now.*" Amanda shut her eyes and forced the two troublemakers out of her head with a deliberate mental block. When blessed quiet reigned for a good long minute, she slowly opened her eyes and thanked a higher power for the silence.

Biting her lower lip, she glanced at the gift-exchange list again, this time contemplating her idea without any extraneous input from the distracting duo. All she wanted was to feel like a seductive, sexy woman and a bit of a bad girl—and know that she was capable of attracting the interest of a man like Christian, even if it was in a secret way.

With confidentiality working in her favor, she could be a little reckless and purchase him a gift that would seduce his mind and body. She could watch his reaction as he opened the present without fear of him ever finding out that she was the one who'd given him something so provocative. It would be like having her own private, sexual interlude with Christian, but without any emotional or physical involvement.

Being his Secret Santa would be safe and fun, for both of them, she thought with a smile. He'd no doubt enjoy the attention and thrill of temptation that came with the present he opened, but like all of his previous relationships, she had no doubt the initial intrigue would eventually fade and he'd forget all about who might have sent him the suggestive holiday gift. And ultimately, no one would ever have to know what she'd done.

Excitement and anticipation blossomed within her, and she had to admit that she liked the sensation that came with being impulsive and adventurous. Before she could change her mind, or Angie and Desiree could reappear with their opinions on the matter, Amanda picked up her pen and jotted Christian's name down on the Secret Santa list.

Right next to her own.

Chapter One

C hristian hustled down the corridor toward the office of Douglas Creighton, the owner and publisher of *Connoisseur* magazine. He'd been summoned by the big boss, and since there was a promotion dangling on the horizon, he wasn't about to keep him waiting any longer than necessary.

Christian had spent the past eight months trying to repair his tarnished reputation after the disastrous incident with Maureen Bowen in the boardroom, and that meant dodging advances from other women in the company who believed he was an easy catch, especially Stacey Roberts, who'd made it her mission to end his oath of celibacy.

He'd worked hard ever since Maureen's departure from the company, dedicating long hours at the office coming up with new and innovative sales strategies that had catapulted him to the number-one sales executive for the past six months in a row. He'd instantly turned down invitations to join his buddies at the local hot spot for a few drinks and an evening of hitting on willing women. He no longer took two-hour pleasure lunches, and the only phone calls he received at work were strictly business. Even his friends were calling him a monk because it had been months since he'd gotten laid.

No doubt about it, he'd cleaned up his act and kept his focus on the job and the possibility of snagging the sales director promotion he wanted so badly. In a few weeks, after Christmas and the first of the year, he'd finally find out if his drive, dedication and respectable way of living had paid off.

As he made his way through the executive floor toward Creighton's wing of offices, he passed a maze of cubicles dominating the center of the twenty-seventh floor of the Jackman Butler Building in New York City, where employees were busy at work. The outer offices flanking the cubicles had amazing views of Manhattan and were reserved for the higher-ups in the company. It was Christian's ultimate goal to earn one of those coveted offices for himself, with floor-to-ceiling windows, paneled walls to hang pictures, and a cherry wood desk large enough to spread out his work without feeling cramped.

He returned his gaze back to where he was going just as Stacey stepped out from her cubicle and deliberately into his path. Her sudden appearance in front of him forced Christian to come to an abrupt halt or collide into her Double Ds, which were one breath away from spilling out of the fur-trimmed bodice of the sexy Mrs. Claus costume she'd worn for the department's holiday party that afternoon. The red velvet mini-dress was formfitting, way too short and no doubt had most of the males in the office fantasizing about getting lucky with her for Christmas.

Unfortunately, Stacey had her sights set on *him,* and he wasn't interested. He'd thwarted her advances more times than he could count, but she gave the words *determination* and *persistence* new meaning. She was just too easy, and despite his own bad-boy reputation, he realized that he'd changed over the past eight months. He'd become more particular and discriminating, and less promiscuous. Somewhere along the way, he'd developed standards and overly assertive women like Stacey no longer appealed to him.

Still, he smiled at her because there was no sense in making an enemy out of the woman by outright telling her how he felt. He did, after all, have to work with her every day. "Cute outfit, Stace. I'm sure you'll be a big hit at the party today."

"I'm glad you like it," she said as her fingers toyed with the white furry ball hanging from the tip of her red velvet Santa hat. "Care to jingle my bells?" She jiggled her breasts, and the two little silver bells attached to the bow barely securing the front of her dress made a light tinkling sound.

He wasn't about to touch that double entendre. "Uh, sorry, but I'll have to pass. If I don't hustle, I'm going to be late for my meeting with Douglas."

"You're no fun anymore, Christian," she said, her cherry-red lips forming a sultry pout. "You know what they say about all work and no play…"

Yeah, it would hopefully give him the promotion he was after. "I'm sure I'll have fun at the holiday party this afternoon."

She brightened considerably at the mention of the department's get-together. "That's right. We're exchanging Secret Santa gifts." She ran her index finger down the front of his tie and leaned in close. "If you'll let me be your secret Santa Claus, I promise to give you a gift guaranteed to blow your mind, among other things," she added suggestively.

Jee-suz. Could the woman be any more forthright? At one time her blatant approach might have interested him, but now he just felt trapped. The need to escape, and fast, overwhelmed him. "Uh, thanks, I'll remember that."

"Ummm, be sure that you do."

Before she could proposition him again, he stepped around her and made a quick getaway. Only then did he notice that they'd had an avid audience who'd witnessed the entire exchange.

Great. Just great.

The guys in the department were shaking their heads in disappointment, as if they couldn't believe he'd turned down a sure thing. And then there was Drew, who was openly gay, and was grinning at Christian in that flirtatious, come-to-daddy way of his.

Christian shuddered. He wasn't homophobic and worked with Drew without any problems. He even considered him a friend, of sorts. But he was uncomfortable with the other guys' jokes that if Christian ever decided to stray to the *other* side, Drew had first dibs on him.

No way. No how. Christian was heterosexual all the way, and he was just on hiatus from dating at the moment to focus on his career. Who knew being celibate would be so difficult, and would compromise his manhood in the process, for crying out loud?

Shaking his head, he bee-lined it down the long corridor that led to the executive suite that was Douglas Creighton's office. He walked past a long panel of glass on the right-hand side, which framed Amanda Creighton's office and mini-suite—a great perk for being the executive editor of *Connoisseur* and heiress to one helluva lucrative publishing company. The floor-to-ceiling window afforded her a modicum of privacy in her inner sanctum, yet allowed her to keep an eye on what was going on outside her office. From what he'd seen, the double doors behind her large desk led to a room furnished with a couch, sitting area, bathroom and even a small kitchenette.

But even though Amanda had been born with the proverbial silver spoon in her mouth, she wasn't a prima donna as most people assumed, based on the first impression Amanda usually gave—of composed sophistication with a reserved personality all wrapped up in a staid, button-up designer suit or outfit. Instead, she was a woman who actually involved herself in all aspects of the company, including contributing her own monthly column, involving herself in various projects and assignments, and generally making sure that everything ran smoothly. She had a way of pitching in without offending anyone, and in the process earned the respect of her co-workers.

Christian came to a stop at her open door. She was standing to the left of her desk at her tall cherry wood filing cabinet, and he lifted his hand to knock just as she pulled out a lower drawer and bent over at the waist to retrieve a file. His hand stilled as he took in the sensual curve of her hips and the sweetly shaped bottom in a pair of tailored black pants.

Awareness hit him hard, and his lower body stirred. The reaction that Stacey had been after made its presence known now—a purely sexual response that reassured him that he was an all-American male who enjoyed women.

But being attracted to the boss's daughter was another thing entirely. Despite how much he might desire this woman, he put the brakes on his thoughts and that glimmer of attraction warming him in private places that had been cold and dormant for too long. Sure, Amanda was very pretty and everything soft and feminine, but there were certain lines in business that a smart man didn't cross. And she had always been one of them. Because her office was also on the executive floor and she was so involved in all aspects of the company, they talked and interacted, but he just never allowed himself to treat her as anything more than a colleague, even if he wished otherwise.

Having found whatever it was she'd been after, Amanda pushed the drawer closed, straightened and turned around holding a file folder in her hand. Her gaze landed on him as he stood in the doorway, and she gasped in surprise.

"Christian," she said, her tone breathless and her face flushed as she pressed a hand to her chest. "I didn't hear you behind me."

Christian never would have considered a turtleneck sweater as a sexy piece of clothing, especially considering how much skin it covered—from beneath her chin, down her arms to her wrists, and all the way to her waist. But that was before he'd seen one on Amanda.

The stretchy knit fabric clung to her upper body like a second skin, and without his permission his gaze dropped briefly to her breasts to take a moment to appreciate the lovely shape of those full, lush mounds outlined to perfection. The bright, festive red color of her sweater complimented her shoulder-length brown hair and made her eyes seem much darker and greener than normal—just as he imagined they'd look in the throes of passion.

What the hell am I thinking?

He mentally shook himself out of his trance and lifted his gaze back to hers. "Sorry about that," he said, unsure if he was apologizing for sneaking up on her, or for ogling her breasts. "I didn't mean to startle you. I was just about to knock. I'm here to see Douglas."

"Oh, of course." She set the file folder down on her desk and appeared as professional and polished as always. If you didn't count the fact that her nipples had tightened and were pressing against the front of her sweater like twin laser beams. An interesting reaction considering it wasn't at all cold in her room.

"He said for you to go on into his office when you arrived," she said, as if her body's response hadn't betrayed her. "He's expecting you."

He nodded. "Great. Thanks." He turned to go,

then something stopped him and he turned back around. "Are you going to be at the holiday party this afternoon?" He had no idea why he asked, or why her answer mattered so much. Maybe it was the attraction he'd always felt toward her, or maybe the hormones that still had his body in an aroused state that were talking for him.

"I wouldn't miss it for anything." She sat down behind her desk and met his gaze with an easy smile. "It should be fun."

Fun. There was that word again. "I was just accused by Stacey of not being any fun, so I better make sure I have a good time at the party."

She laughed lightly, probably because it was a known fact that Stacey had made it her mission to show him her version of fun. "With the Secret Santa gift exchange, the party is bound to be full of surprises."

He leaned casually against the door frame and tipped his head curiously. "So, whose name did you get?"

She lifted a brow, making him feel like a naughty boy for asking. "You know I can't tell you that." Amusement laced her voice.

"You could, if you really wanted to." He pushed his hands into the front pockets of his trousers and grinned persuasively. "It hardly seems fair that you know who everyone else has for a Secret Santa, but no one knows who you have."

Her pretty eyes sparkled mischievously. "Ahhh, that's one of the perks of being in charge of the list. And, I've always been good at keeping secrets." Then she pointed across the way to the big double doors behind Christian. "I do believe Douglas is waiting for you."

He immediately straightened and silently reprimanded himself for getting so caught up in the conversation, for getting so caught up in *Amanda,* that he'd forgotten his original reason for being there.

What the hell had that been all about?

Refusing to analyze that particular question, he turned around and made his way toward Douglas's office. He took a brief moment to collect his composure and thoughts, then knocked twice and entered the spacious room.

The other man glanced up from where he was sitting behind his desk. Douglas was in his mid-sixties, but he was one of those lucky men who had the kind of ageless features and thick, salt-and-pepper hair that belied his age and gave him a distinguished look. His eyes were the same green shade as his daughter's, and held a wealth of wisdom and shrewd intelligence.

Christian closed the distance between them. "You wanted to see me, sir?"

"Yes, I did." Douglas took off his wire-framed glasses, set them on a pile of papers, then waved a hand at the chairs in front of his desk. "Have a seat, Christian."

It wasn't often that he was summoned to Douglas Creighton's office, and considering the last time he'd paid a visit to the big boss had been for scandalous reasons, Christian was hoping this meeting would end on a more positive note.

Settling into one of the seats the other man had indicated, he forced himself to relax. "What can I do for you, Mr. Creighton?"

"Actually, it's what I'd like to do for you." Douglas leaned back in his chair and regarded Christian in that direct manner of his. "I was just reviewing your most recent employee evaluation, and I'm very impressed with your sales performance review, as well as the initiative you've taken lately in various creative approaches that you've used to increase advertising sales in the magazine."

So far, so good, Christian thought. "Thank you."

"It seems you've really put that talent and drive I've always known you possessed to good use. Your hard work, along with all the long hours you've put in at the office has been duly noted." Withdrawing an envelope from the top drawer of his desk, Douglas handed it to Christian. "Here's a holiday bonus based on your review."

The flap wasn't sealed, and Christian took a quick peek at the check inside. He swallowed hard, bowled over by the amount of his bonus. "That's very generous. Thank you."

Douglas nodded. "I always knew you had potential, Christian, given the right incentive and direction. And I want you with the company for a long time to come. You know that the sales director position needs to be filled, and there's a few of you I'm considering for the job. Keep up the good work and we'll see how things go after the first of the year."

Excellent. Now, all Christian had to do was keep himself on the straight and narrow for the next two weeks, and one of those outer offices with a view of Manhattan might just be his after all.

Festive and *fun* definitely described the department's holiday party later that afternoon. Considering how Christian's meeting had gone with Douglas, he was in a fantastic mood and ready to enjoy himself for a few hours.

Everyone on the executive floor was gathered in the reception area where a small three-foot Christmas tree had been placed. The fake green branches were weighted down with silver tinsel, swags of garish garland and bright ornaments. Beneath the tree was a slew of gaily wrapped presents waiting to be opened.

A table had been set up with holiday sweets and potluck style offerings, and Christian had already indulged way past his normal limit. Eggnog, hot spiced cider and lively conversation flowed freely, mingling with lots of revelry and good cheer. An abundance of mistletoe that someone had hung in strategic places around the room added to the entertainment, but Christian steered clear of those sprigs of trouble. He had no desire to get caught in a compromising position with Stacey, or anyone else for that matter.

Then there was comedic Drew, who'd attached a sprig of mistletoe to the front of his slacks as a joke, but as yet no one had taken him up on the offer to plant a kiss there. When Drew crooked his finger Christian's way, he merely laughed and shook his head at the other man's outrageous humor.

"Okay, everyone, take your seats," Stacey announced excitedly, clapping her hands to get the group's attention. "It's time for the gift exchange."

Christian found an empty chair and sat down across from where Amanda was seated. They exchanged smiles before Jason, the guy sitting next to her, said something and she started talking to him. That was okay with Christian because it gave him a few moments to watch her interact with the other man. His gaze took in her profile and the classic features that made up her lovely face. He watched her sensual lips as they moved, the way her green eyes sparkled with genuine sincerity, and the breathy, lighthearted way she laughed.

He felt that familiar tug of awareness and glanced away before it slipped beyond his control. For the past five years that he'd worked with Amanda, Christian had always found her attractive in a very soft and subdued way—quite the opposite of the bold and willing women he'd hooked up with in the past. But in his head, he'd always known that she was way out of his league. She still was, considering who her father was, and he'd do well to remember that before he did something incredibly stupid—like ask her out on a date.

Yeah, like someone of her caliber would be interested in a playboy like you!

He pushed the thought from his mind and returned his attention to the party. Someone had brought a CD of holiday songs, and strains of "Here Comes Santa Claus" filled the reception area. Christian looked up and saw *Mrs.* Santa Claus, coming straight toward where he was sitting with an I'm-going-to-eat-you-up smile on her lips. She bent low, giving him an unwanted view of her ample cleavage, and flashed her white ruffled panties to everyone behind her as she handed him the long, slim wrapped box she was delivering.

"This present is for you," Stacey said, licking her lips in a way he found much too tawdry for his taste. "And just so you know, you can unwrap me anytime, anywhere."

She walked away with a deliberate sashay of her hips, and he groaned, certain she was his penance for his own past promiscuous behavior. The good news was she made him realize that he had no desire to go back to that shallow, superficial way of living.

The gift exchange began, with everyone taking a turn to open their presents. Jason received an engraved money clip, and Drew was thrilled to get the DVD gift set of his favorite movie, *Broke-back Mountain.* Someone gave Amanda a set of her favorite Victoria's Secret bath products, and Stacey wasn't at all ashamed to show everyone the racy G-string panties her Secret Santa had bought for her. In fact, Christian was surprised that she didn't offer to model the barely there undies for everyone to see.

Before long, it was Christian's turn. He ripped the wrapping paper off his gift, lifted the lid and found a nice, dignified blue-and-gray striped tie inside. Nothing wild and crazy or embarrassing, thank God. Tucked between the tie and tissue paper was a small white envelope, and he picked it up. Undeniably curious, he withdrew the plain white note card inside and read the typed message.

At first glance, this tie may seem like a respectable gift. And it is, if you wear it to work. But if you were my lover, I'd use this gift to tie you up so I could do all the things I've fantasized about doing to you for a long time now. I want to tease you, and please you, and make you lose control. Will you let me do those things to you?

Hell, yes. He was so caught up in the moment that the answer came way too easily. Oh, yeah, he was definitely intrigued.

Realizing that the note had actually aroused him, in more ways than one, he kept the box on his lap and dared to glance up. A dozen pairs of eyes were watching him, and he realized that there were only a couple of people in this room that he could think of who would have the nerve to send him such a suggestive note.

"Mmmm, nice tie," Stacey said appreciatively, and he had no doubt that *she'd* tie him up given the chance.

"I agree," Drew said, adding his fashion sense to the conversation, along with a wink at Christian. "Blue and gray look good on you and really bring out the color of your eyes."

Oh, God. Had Drew fantasized about gazing into his eyes while Christian was tied to his bed? Had he just gotten turned on by a gay guy's propensity for bondage? The notion shriveled his arousal.

Desperate for answers, he searched other faces for some kind of clue, but most everyone's attention had moved on to the next person who was opening their gift. Everyone but Amanda, who looked at him with amusement and was trying not to laugh at Drew's girlie comment.

At least, that was what he assumed until a sudden realization dawned on him. Amanda was the list keeper, the one and only person who knew exactly who'd given him the gift. And he knew he was going to drive himself insane trying to figure out who his secret admirer was. Because there weren't many people in this room that he wanted to get down and dirty with, and now that he had this tie and provocative note hanging over his head, he was going to be constantly second-guessing certain people's motives, comments and suggestions.

He couldn't afford that kind of distraction right now, not with the promotion and corner office almost his. No matter what it took, he had to get Amanda to reveal who his Secret Santa was.

Chapter Two

Well, that was certainly interesting, Desiree said, appearing on Amanda's left shoulder to make her opinion known.

Amanda carried a few empty bowls from the potluck into the break room in an attempt to clean up after the party, as well as to escape the speculative stare Christian had been tossing her way for the past half hour. She had no idea why he was watching her so intently, but his attention was starting to unnerve her.

Interesting was definitely one way to describe his reaction to her gift. When he'd first opened the present she'd bought for him, he'd looked relieved that he hadn't received some kind of outrageous gag gift. Then he'd read the note she'd tucked between the tissue paper and the tie. From across the room she'd watched his expression shift from pleasant surprise to fascination. She had to admit that the slow, sexy smile that had curved his lips as he'd read her intimate message had given her a small thrill. Oh, she'd definitely managed to get under his skin, until he glanced up, scoured the room with his gaze and his initial excitement gave way to full-blown panic.

Amanda set the bowls in the sink and filled them with warm, soapy water. She had no idea what had triggered the latter response, and now, for some reason, he had *her* set in his sights. So, she figured the best thing to do was hide out until the party was completely over. Already, employees were heading back to their cubicles and offices to pack up for the weekend, so it was only a matter of time before Christian left, as well. With luck, the naughty note she'd sent to him would no doubt be forgotten by Tuesday morning, after Christmas had come and gone.

I don't have a very good feeling about this, Angie said, wringing her hands anxiously in her lap.

Stop being such a worrywart. Desiree scowled at her nemesis for putting a damper on the fun. *Christian loved the gift and sexy note. Now, if only Amanda had the nerve to follow through on that little fantasy of hers, she'd be one happy and very satisfied woman, I'm sure.*

Annoyed with the bickering, Amanda shook her head as she turned off the faucet, then grabbed a towel to dry her hands. "Go away. The two of you are driving me crazy."

"Who is driving you crazy?"

Startled by the sound of Christian's voice behind

her—the second time in the same day, no less—
Amanda spun around to face him. He stood just inside
the break room, looking gorgeous as always with his
tousled hair, intense blue eyes and lean, honed body
she'd imagined naked far too many times. A small
frown creased his dark brows as he waited for her to
answer his question.

God, he's so hot. Desiree sighed and fanned herself
with her hand. *If you're not going to take advantage of all
that studliness, introduce me and I'll do it for you.*

If Amanda had the ability to knock the cheeky
devil off her shoulder, she would have. Instead, she
ignored Desiree and her outrageous request. "Uh,
nobody. I was, uh, just talking to myself."

"Oh." He pushed his fingers through his already
disheveled hair, his expression troubled, which wasn't
something she'd ever associated with Christian, who
was always the epitome of self-confidence. "Look, I
need to talk to you."

That doesn't sound good at all, Angie said, much too
nervously for Amanda's liking. *I warned you that sending
him that gift wasn't a good idea!*

Amanda pushed Angie and her ominous words out
of her head, refusing to allow her guardian angel's
apprehension to become her own. Placing the terry
towel on the counter, she smiled at Christian as if
nothing was wrong. "Sure. What's up?"

He released a tension-filled breath. "I need to see the Secret Santa list."

Uh-oh, Angie muttered.

Amanda kept her outward composure cool and calm, but inside she had to admit to her first little niggle of uneasiness. "Christian, you know I can't show you the list."

His lean jaw clenched. "Then I need to know who had my name."

She shook her head. "I can't tell you that, either."

Gaze narrowed, he walked across the break room, slowly closing the distance between them. "Yes, you can."

"No, I can't." She took a step back and let out a small squeak of surprise when her back connected with the edge of the counter behind her.

Finally, he stopped in front of her—a respectable distance away for two colleagues engaging in a discussion, but his nearness affected Amanda on too many levels anyways. She could smell the warm, male scent of his cologne and feel the heat emanating from him. Her keen awareness of him as a man, not to mention those sensual lips of his, did crazy things to her hormones and made her weak in the knees.

Thinking fast, she changed the direction of the conversation. "Is there a problem with your tie? Because I can ask the person who gave it to you for a gift receipt so you can exchange it for something else."

"No, the tie itself is fine."

"Then what's wrong?" she asked, but knew exactly what had set him off—her written fantasy.

He hesitated a moment, then shoved his hands into the front pockets of his trousers before saying, "There was a note that came with the gift, and I need to know who wrote it."

Her heart beat so hard and fast in her chest, she was surprised it didn't show against her sweater. "Was the note offensive?" It was hard to believe that an experienced guy like Christian would be repulsed by the provocative message she'd penned for him, so she was guessing that he was just out to appease his curiosity.

But how far would he go to satisfy his need to know? she wondered, and felt a tiny shiver course down her spine.

"It all depends on who wrote it," he said, frustration deepening the tone of his voice. "There are two people who seem the most likely, and well, let's just say that if I know who sent me that note I can at least watch my back."

The innuendo in his comment, along with the slight bit of humor curving the corner of his mouth told Amanda that one of those people he suspected of writing the note was Drew. And, undoubtedly, the other was Stacey because the office bimbo had made her interest in Christian openly obvious over the past few months.

Laughter and voices traveled into the break room from the reception area, and Christian cast a quick glance over his shoulder to make sure they were still alone before returning his attention back to Amanda. He leaned close, his gaze holding a hint of desperation as he pressed his advantage in low, urgent tones. "I swear, if you tell me who my Secret Santa is, I'll keep the information to myself. No one will ever know that you told me anything."

She really had shaken him up with that note, more than Amanda had ever believed was possible. Now, it was more imperative than ever that he never find out that she was the one who'd penned the fantasy because it could make things awkward between them and ultimately change the dynamics of their working relationship.

I hate to tell you that I told you so, Angie whispered in her ear, *but I did tell you so!*

Feeling trapped between the counter, Christian's gorgeous body and her own deceit, Amanda felt the overwhelming need for space and breathing room. Forcing her feet to *move,* she stepped around the man in front of her.

"I'm really sorry, Christian. Everyone trusts me

with that list, and it's up to each individual person to decide whether or not they want their recipient to know they were their Secret Santa." She gave him her best apologetic look. "I just can't break confidence that way."

As if finally accepting that she wasn't going to cave to his request, he exhaled a deep breath and gave up the fight. "Fine." The one word was rife with exasperation, but there was a determination burning in his gaze that contradicted his acquiescence.

Without another word, he turned and left the break room, and that uneasy feeling in the pit of her belly grew.

Wow, you really did a number on him, Desiree said with a proud smile on her red lips. *I didn't think you had it in you. I'm very proud of you, girl.*

Amanda placed a hand on her churning stomach, trying without success to calm that unsettling sensation spreading through her. She'd wanted a reaction out of him, and she'd gotten that, and probably a whole lot more than she'd bargained for. Lord help her if Christian ever discovered that she was the one responsible for the gift he'd received and the tantalizing note that had piqued more than just his curiosity.

The Lord has nothing to do with this mess you and Desiree made of things, Angie said primly as her halo gleamed a bright, shiny gold over her head. *I really do think you're on your own with this one.*

Amanda was afraid that Angie was right.

Christian was beginning to think that Amanda wasn't ever going to leave for the evening, and he was starting to feel like a stalker considering the way he was staking out her office from the meeting room across the way. The light was off in the room he was in, and he was able to remain out of sight while keeping an eye on Amanda through the glass partition. Still, he'd been in there for an hour, and he was quickly growing impatient and restless.

However, he had to admit that he was enjoying being able to watch Amanda on the sly. Believing she was completely alone in the office after six o'clock on a Friday night of a holiday weekend, she was very relaxed and at ease. The reserve and poise that surrounded her during business hours was now stripped away, revealing a woman who was much softer and more laid-back than she let anyone at the office see.

As executive editor and the daughter of a publishing mogul, she had to keep up a strong and competent front with her co-workers, to prove she could handle the pressures and stress of the job, as well as everyone else. And she managed the feat quite well because no one ever questioned her dedication, or the fact that she deserved to follow in her father's footsteps. Her commitment and loyalty, as well as her ability to handle any crises with finesse, spoke for itself.

But as she moved around her desk with a natural grace, he had to admit that this open, unconstrained side to Amanda tempted him. As did the stunningly sensual curves of her body, and that rich, brown hair that looked so soft and inviting beneath the lights in her office. When she absently ran her tongue across her bottom lip, his mind veered off on a tangent of its own, imagining that sweet mouth beneath his, all hot and damp and eager just for him.

From there, the scenario spun out of control, taking him places he had no business traveling with Amanda, even if it was all in his mind. Places like his bed, and having her gloriously naked and wonderfully wanton in it. With him restrained by a blue-and-gray striped tie and Amanda teasing him, pleasing him and making him lose control…

The words from the note he'd received with his gift earlier today played into his fantasy, giving him a much needed jolt of reality and reminding him why he was hiding out in the meeting room. And it wasn't because he'd suddenly become a voyeur, though the erection straining against the fly of his slacks begged to differ.

After confronting Amanda in the break room and

getting nothing for his efforts, he'd decided that there was only one thing left for him to do. Sneak into her office after everyone was gone for the night and find that damnable Secret Santa list.

Jesus, he was so pathetic. And desperate to discover who was yanking his chain with that provocative note.

Forever seemed to pass before Amanda finally tossed a few things into her briefcase, snapped it closed, then put on her black wool coat, leaving it unbuttoned despite the evening chill awaiting her. Grabbing her purse and briefcase, she locked her office door, switched off the main lights, then headed for the elevator that would take her down to the private garage where she parked her car.

As soon as the elevator door closed behind Amanda, Christian made his move. Jimmying her office door open was ridiculously easy since it wasn't a bolt lock. A slow, careful slide of a thin credit card released the latch, and that easily, he was in.

He turned the light back on and began searching her desk for the list, feeling a tad guilty for breaking and entering, not to mention shuffling through Amanda's things. To ease his conscience, he didn't linger on any one thing and kept his focus on his search.

Everything was neat and tidy, like the woman herself, making the task of looking for the list a quick process. Unfortunately, what he was looking for wasn't to be found in her desk drawers. Frustration got the best of him, and he swore out loud, refusing to admit defeat just yet.

Hands on his hips, he glanced around the office, and his gaze came to a stop on the filing cabinets. Figuring it was worth a look, he checked the private files under *S* for *Secret Santa,* and laughed out loud when he found one labeled with that exact title. Leave it to Amanda to be so predictable.

Tucked inside was the handwritten list he'd been after. Feeling triumphant, he withdrew the paper and his gaze immediately zeroed in on his name, which was right beside the name of the one person he never would have suspected of doing something so bold.

Amanda Creighton.

"Jees-uz," he muttered beneath his breath, unable to believe that Miss Prim and Proper had penned such an arousing and seductive fantasy—to him. Knowingly. Deliberately. And with the certainty that he'd never discover the truth. Was it no wonder that she wouldn't let him take a peek?

Now he understood why, and her involvement certainly put an interesting and unexpected twist on things. It also made his attraction to her very real because the desire was obviously reciprocated on her end, as well. Try as he might, he couldn't ignore the warm flare of arousal that had begun to radiate through him at the mental image of Amanda tying him up for their mutual pleasure and satisfaction.

The big question was, what was he going to do about the incriminating information he'd just uncovered, as well as the tie and brazen note she'd given him? If he was a smart man, he'd slip the Secret Santa file right back into the cabinet, pretend he never saw that list, and forget about Amanda and her erotic, mind-blowing fantasy involving him.

"What do you think you're doing?"

The sound of Amanda's indignant question jarred Christian out of his thoughts and made him jump from her unexpected presence. Still holding the list in his hand, he turned around to face the woman standing in the doorway of her office. Her eyes were wide as she stared at him, and the flush sweeping across her complexion combined shock, panic...and a flash of guilt.

So much for being a smart man and getting out while the getting had been good. Now, he didn't have that option. Caught red-handed with no escape, Christian figured there was only one thing left for him to do—confront Amanda with the evidence he'd unearthed and teach her a little lesson about what could happen when you teased a man beyond his limits.

Oh, yeah, now this is getting good! From Amanda's left shoulder, Desiree rubbed her hands together and her eyes sparkled with anticipation, taking obvious delight in the recent turn of events.

Amanda, on the other hand, was mortified to find Christian in her office—the Secret Santa list clutched between his long fingers. She'd definitely startled him, but he didn't look at all worried about being caught in the act. In fact, there was a certain smugness about him that caused a frisson of awareness to take hold.

And judging by the satisfied look in his eyes, there was no doubt in her mind that he was now well aware that *she'd* given him that very intimate note.

What did you expect? Angie scolded, like the mother Amanda had lost at such a young age. *When you play with fire you're bound to get burned.*

If that's the case, then burn me, baby, Desiree said in a low, sultry purr that was directed Christian's way.

Ha! Angie crossed her arms over her chest. *You're so used to the heat, you have no idea what it's like to be burned!*

You're just jealous that I like it hot. Desiree smirked.

Stop, both of you! Amanda gave her head a hard shake. *I can't think straight with the two of you squabbling in my mind!*

The voices went quiet, but Amanda knew the reprieve was only temporary. Neither Angie nor Desiree was about to miss this showdown between her and Christian.

When Amanda had gotten down to her car and realized she'd forgotten a file for an article she planned on editing over the holiday weekend, she'd never have imagined that a quick trip back up to her office would turn into a confrontation she had no wish to have with Christian. But other than ignoring the fact that he'd broken into her office and gone through her personal files, she didn't have much choice.

She just hoped and prayed that she'd be able to get out of this very awkward situation with her pride intact.

"I asked you what you were doing in here," she said, lifting her chin in a show of authority.

"Well, now, that should be obvious," he said in a slow, lazy drawl that had way too much of an effect on Amanda's sorely neglected libido. "I'm getting the answer that you weren't willing to give me earlier in the break room. With good reason, it seems, considering *you're* my Secret Santa."

Despite that truth, there was no way she was going to let him get the upper hand. Squaring her shoulders, she strode into the room and right up to Christian, focusing on a more condemning issue that involved him. "You broke into my office. I could have you written up for that, or even fired."

An infuriatingly sexy smile curved up the corner of his lips. "But you won't do either."

She arched a brow. "And what makes you so sure about that?"

He leaned a shoulder against her file cabinets, making himself comfortable. "For starters, I have a list right here in my hand showing that you're my Secret Santa."

Unimpressed, she shrugged. "So?"

"I also have a very suggestive note from you, which if brought to light, could be misconstrued in many ways."

Hearing the idle threat in his words, she narrowed her gaze. "Such as?"

"Let's see," he said, taking a moment to think as his eyes glimmered with amusement. "There's always sexual harassment."

She opened her mouth, then snapped it shut again. He was toying with her, just as she'd toyed with him. And he was enjoying every minute of it. "Oh, that's a rich claim, coming from the office bad boy."

"Hey, I've been a very good boy for months now," he said, affecting a virtuous look that would have made Angie proud. "And I'm quite sure that your father would be absolutely appalled to find out his daughter wrote such a naughty letter to me."

"Ohhhh, you're a rat!" Her hands clenched into

fists at her sides, even though she knew that she was to blame for riling him in the first place with that tie and note. This whole entire mess was her fault, but that didn't mean she was going to let Christian have any kind of advantage over her.

"Give me that list." She held out her hand.

"Nope." He folded the piece of paper in half, then in another half, making a tidy square. "It's my security deposit. You get me for breaking and entering, and I have the Secret Santa list and a very sexy note to go with it."

She gasped in shock. "That's blackmail."

"Hmmm." He grinned shamelessly and winked at her, exuding way too much charm for her peace of mind. "Sure, if that's what you want to call it."

She made a quick grab for the folded paper, but he was quicker. He held it just out of her grasp, and unless she wanted to plaster her body against his to reach the list, she was out of luck. It was an appealing thought, but she didn't want to end up in a wrestling match with him, no matter how much Desiree would enjoy being a spectator to that sport.

"Give it back, Christian." She used a firm, no-nonsense tone that usually got her exactly what she wanted.

Not today and not with Christian. "If you want it that badly, you'll have to get it yourself." He slid the folded list down the front of his pants, his gaze brimming with a wicked challenge. "That is, if you dare."

Stunned by his audacity, she gaped at him, though she couldn't deny that the tips of her fingers tingled at the thought of chasing after that paper. Heat flushed across her cheeks and down her body, making her wool coat feel suffocating and unbearably warm.

He laughed, a low, rich chuckle that slid down her spine like a silky caress and increased her awareness of him. "I didn't think so. Afraid you might just get more than you bargained for?"

Oh, yeah. "You're a cad."

"I've certainly been called worse." He crossed his arms over his chest and regarded her with mild curiosity. "But you, Ms. Creighton, are a tease. What was that tie and note about, anyway?"

The shocking truth lodged in her throat, and thankfully a quick, logical explanation popped into her head. "It was a joke, okay?" One that had taken a turn she never would have anticipated.

"A joke," he said, repeating her words and looking as though he were mulling over her response. "Was it because you wanted to get me all hot and bothered?"

Her heart skipped a beat at his too-accurate guess. "Of course not!" she managed to sputter. For a woman who always kept her emotions in check, especially at work, this man had a way of flustering her from head to toe.

You wouldn't be in this situation if you'd just listened to me, Angie whispered. *But nooo, you were weak and let Desiree lead you over to the dark side.*

"Well, just in case you're curious, it did get me all hot and bothered," he said, humor and something far sexier lacing his voice. "That is, until the possibility crossed my mind that either Stacey or Drew had given me such a provocative gift." He shuddered for effect, telling Amanda without words how he felt about those two scenarios.

A burst of laughter escaped her before she could stop it, relieving a bit of the nervous tension pulling tight within her. In a way she'd never admit to him, she now better understood his desperate need to find out who his Secret Santa was.

"You find that funny?" He tried to appear stern, but couldn't hide the mirth flickering in his gaze.

She pressed her fingers to her lips to hold in her laughter, but couldn't stop another residual chuckle. "It really is funny when you think about it. Especially with Drew."

"I'm glad you're so amused." Pushing away from the file cabinet, he moved toward her and stopped less than a foot away. "As for me, I'm much more in-trigued by the fact that you sent me that tie, and wrote me that note." Lifting his hand, he grazed his thumb along the line of her jaw, while his fingers dipped just inside the high collar of her sweater and caressed the side of her neck. "Why did you do it, Amanda?" he asked huskily.

Her pulse tripped all over itself at his sensual touch, and her nipples tightened into hard peaks, aching for the same kind of intimate attention. She inched backward to break the contact, and her bottom connected with the edge of her desk.

"I told you, it was a joke," she said lightly. "A gag gift."

"Liar," he chided softly. Slowly, he closed the distance between them once again, and she knew just by looking into his dark, determined eyes that he wouldn't let her escape him so easily a second time. "I think you're secretly attracted to me."

Instinctively, she pressed a hand to his chest to hold him off, and immediately realized her mistake when she felt the solid heat and strength of his body beneath her fingers. Her *attraction,* the one she was just about to deny, flared into full-blown desire. She struggled to breathe, and when she finally did manage to inhale, she drew in the heady scent of sandalwood and aroused male.

She swallowed back a needy groan. Feeling her physical response to him slipping a few critical notches, she kept her hand splayed on his chest and grasped for control. "Don't flatter yourself, Casanova," she said with a sassy toss of her head. "Attraction has nothing to do with it."

"Oh, really?" A too-perceptive smile eased up the corner of his tempting mouth as he slipped his hand inside her coat and boldly settled his large palm on her hip. "If you're not attracted to me, then why are you trembling?"

She rolled her eyes, pretending indifference, which wasn't an easy feat when everything about Christian made her acutely sensitive to just how alone the two of them were in the office building. "You're obviously imagining things."

"Am I?" He tipped his head, studying her like a man who had all the time in the world, and planned to use every minute to make her squirm. "Maybe we ought to put the attraction theory to a little test."

She frowned, immediately wary. "What kind of test?"

Instead of responding verbally, he used the slow, gradual press of his body against hers to make his point, proving he was a man of action rather than words when it came to getting a woman's attention. Their hips and thighs met, and the curve of her bottom caught on the edge of her desk. Sliding the fingers of his free hand into her hair, he cupped the back of her head in his palm. He gave a small, light, arousing tug on the strands tangled around his fingers, forcing her face to tip up toward his.

His gaze was hypnotic as it stared into hers. Dark and hot, and filled with all kinds of sinful intent.

The heat alone was enough to make her melt from the inside out. Between the hard, powerful body aligned against hers like a familiar lover, and the strong male hands anchoring her even more securely to the spot, she felt breathlessly excited, and a whole lot out of her element when it came to this kind of situation.

"What…" Her voice rasped, and she swallowed to clear her throat, though it was impossible to steady her erratic pulse. "What are you doing?"

"That should be obvious." His lashes fell half-mast over his eyes, and his mouth eased into a slumberous smile, making him all the more sexy and appealing. "I'm putting your 'I'm-not-attracted-to-you' claim to the test. So far, you seem to be failing."

He lowered his head toward hers, and a swell of panic rose within her. She curled her fingers into the fabric of his shirt, knowing that if his lips so much as touched hers, she'd be a goner. Putty in his hands to do with as he wished. She knew he was just playing with her, attempting to get even for the gift and note she'd given him, and that was reason enough to put a halt to this crazy situation.

"Christian," she said firmly, trying to put him off, except a soft, sultry, telltale moan followed his name.

His lips skimmed along her cheek to her ear, and nuzzled that sensitive spot beneath the lobe that made her shiver and increased the rapid beat of her heart. "Shhh," he whispered, his breath feathering warm and damp against her skin. "This test won't hurt a bit. I promise."

That was what she was most afraid of—receiving too much pleasure only to have him leave her craving so much more.

Go for it, Amanda. Desiree urged, her enthusiasm unmistakable. *You know you want to.*

Oh, yes, I do. So why was she fighting what she wanted so badly? Who cared that he was out to extract a bit of retribution, especially when he was offering such an erotic form of revenge? Tossing aside any last misgivings, she decided to seize the moment, enjoy the kiss and whatever else Christian was willing to give.

Closing her eyes, she turned her head, seeking the warmth of his mouth with her own. Their lips met, his firm and sensual as they claimed hers and took control of the kiss. Reaching up, she tunneled her fingers into his thick, silky hair and opened to him, to the dampness and heat and the slow, deep stroke of his tongue.

The hands on her hips tightened as he pressed his lower body closer, harder, against hers in a slow, grinding thrust that made her moan deep in her throat. Shamelessly, she strained beneath the delicious assault, and as if knowing exactly what she needed, he slid his hands around to her bottom and lifted her so that she was sitting on the surface of her desk. He nudged her knees wide apart and moved in between her legs, branding her with the unmistakable pressure and friction of his rock-hard erection rubbing against the sensitive place between her thighs.

His mouth slanted across hers in a more provocative, dominating kiss, dragging her deeper under his spell and possessing her in a primitive, sexual way that was new and exciting to her. She was used to polite, courteous sex, not this explosion of aggression and heat that threatened to consume her.

She wrapped her legs around the back of his thighs and embraced the electrifying sensation. Desire began to flow through her veins, liquid and hot. Down to her aching breasts. Swirling in her belly. Making her sex weep for the pulsing, driving force of him sliding deep, deep inside her. Seemingly of their own accord, her hands slid down his chest and grazed the belt buckle securing the front of his pants.

Abruptly, he broke the kiss and jerked back, his expression stunned. He was breathing hard, his eyes dark and glazed with lust, and it took extreme effort on Amanda's part not to pull him back and make him finish what he'd just started.

From her left shoulder, Desiree applauded her efforts. *It's about time. I was starting to worry about you.*

Christian swore beneath his breath and stepped farther away from Amanda, breaking all physical contact and leaving her sitting on the desk. A dark, troubled frown creased his brows and a muscle in his jaw ticked. In a carefully controlled voice that still held an underlying rasp of arousal, he said, "I need to get the hell out of here before we do something we'll both regret."

With that, he turned and walked out of her office, leaving her alone and very confused about what had just happened between them. Considering their working relationship, and Christian's love 'em and leave 'em reputation, she ought to be grateful that at least he'd been thinking clearly enough to stop things before they'd escalated to the point of no return.

But she wasn't grateful. She was disappointed.

Wow, the man certainly knows how to kiss, among other things, Desiree said breathlessly.

Even Angie fanned herself, a pink blush sweeping across her cheeks. Despite that, she still managed to put everything back into perspective, as was her job as Amanda's guardian angel. *Of course he does. He's had a whole lot of experience.*

Experience is a very good thing, Desiree retorted with a

sly smile.

Amanda dragged a shaky hand through her hair and stood on less-than-steady legs. "Yeah, well, it doesn't seem to matter now. He got exactly what he wanted, and now it's over."

He'd taken the list for safekeeping, and a kiss for revenge. An erotic, bone-melting kiss that would haunt her dreams for a long time to come.

Chapter Three

Christian slid the blue-and-gray striped tie between his fingers as he paced a restless path in his living room and thought about what had happened between him and Amanda just a few hours ago, a kiss that had literally rocked his world and left him wanting her with an intensity he couldn't shake.

He'd only meant to teach Amanda a lesson. To show her that when you teased a bear with something he wanted, you were bound to get bitten. But instead, all he'd managed to do was unleash a desire that she clearly felt as well, and it had taken every ounce of strength he possessed not to take her right then and there on her desk.

Lord knew, she'd been soft and warm and more than willing. Just remembering the way she'd wrapped her legs around his hips and responded so wantonly to their embrace made him rock-hard all over again.

The big question was, what was he going to do about their mutual lust? *Absolutely nothing,* should have been his immediate response. He'd walked away from her earlier with every intention of never touching her again. He'd meant what he'd said about regrets, and they did have their working relationship to consider, not to mention his promotion that was still up in the air.

But now, after rereading her sexy note and contemplating all the sensual pleasures the two of them could no doubt share, he couldn't help but wonder if making love to Amanda, and taking her up on her Secret Santa gift, was worth the possible risks.

Yes. That particular answer came much too easily, and he wasn't about to refuse something he wanted so badly. After all, they were consenting adults and were completely capable of indulging in a brief, private affair outside of the office. Judging by Amanda's attempt to keep her gift to him a secret, he was certain she'd welcome a mutual agreement to keep their relationship just between the two of them.

For the first time in hours, Christian grinned, feeling like a man on a mission. Amanda wanted to tie him up and have her way with him? No problem, he thought, as he slipped the tie she'd given him around the collar of his shirt and secured it into a loose knot against his throat.

He was up for any kind of erotic, sexual games she wanted to play.

✧　✧　✧

It really is for the best that Christian walked away before things went too far between the two of you.

Neither Angie's voice of reason nor the pint of Ben & Jerry's Chocolate Fudge Brownie ice cream she was spooning into her mouth could console Amanda and her dismal mood. Even the new, sexy, bright red Jimmy Choo heels she'd slipped on after a long, hot bath did nothing to lift her spirits. More depressed than before, she tucked her legs beneath her on the couch so she didn't have to stare at the pretty strappy shoes that would most likely never see the light of day. Just like all the others in her collection.

She closed her eyes and groaned. If Ben & Jerry's and a beautiful pair of expensive shoes couldn't cure Amanda's blues, she was in worse shape than she'd realized. Sure, she'd been devastated when Christian had kissed her senseless then dismissed the incident because he was afraid of regrets, but she never would have imagined that she'd feel so rejected. So alone and wondering if any other man would ever live up to that amazingly seductive kiss.

Even now, hours after the fact, she still felt on edge and restless in a way that would no doubt keep her tossing and turning for the entire night. Christian had started a craving in her, then had left her aroused and wanting more. More of his drugging kisses, his sensual touch, his strong, hard body pressed against hers. Preferably with both of them completely naked.

But that wasn't going to happen, she knew, and shoveled another bite of chocolate fudge brownie into her mouth. He'd made his feelings about the situation abundantly clear, and just like every other woman he tangled with, she was yet another casualty of his charm.

Well, that was what she got for ignoring Angie's warning and sending Christian that Secret Santa gift in the first place. She truly had no one but herself to blame for the entire fiasco.

Her apartment phone rang, interrupting her thoughts. The distinct ring tone told her it was the doorman downstairs calling. Picking up the extension on the end table next to the couch, she answered with the most upbeat voice she could muster. "Hello?"

"Good evening, Ms. Creighton," William replied in his normal businesslike tone. "There's a gentleman by the name of Christian Miller here to see you. Shall I send him up to your place?"

Shocked by the unexpected announcement, Amanda's mind spun. He'd obviously gotten her address from the company roster, but after the tense way they'd parted company at the office, she couldn't begin to imagine his reasons for being at her place now. To apologize, maybe? To return the tie he had no intention of ever wearing?

"Ms. Creighton?" William prompted after too many silent seconds had passed.

She shook herself from her stupor and replied. "I, uh, yes, of course. Send him on up."

She hung up the phone, not sure what to do first. She had about a minute before he arrived. Quickly, she took her Ben & Jerry's back to the kitchen and put the rest of the pint into the freezer. Then she ran her fingers through her still-damp and tousled hair, wishing she'd dried it tonight. Wishing, too, that she had more time to prepare herself, mentally and physically, for Christian's spontaneous visit.

But she didn't. Her doorbell rang and a dozen butterflies took flight in her stomach as she headed toward the entryway. The heels of her Jimmy Choos clicked on the marble floor, and she groaned when she thought about how odd she probably looked in her drawstring pajama pants imprinted with bright red lips, a matching cotton camisole top…and a pair of racy red shoes with a four-inch heel.

The doorbell rang again, followed by a brisk, impatient knock, leaving her no time to unfasten the double straps wrapped around each ankle to take the shoes off. So, she opened the door and faced the man who'd rejected her just a few hours before.

He stood on the other side of the threshold, looking incredibly gorgeous, with his dark, disheveled hair and those deep blue eyes that took in her pajamas in a slow, sweeping glance. The sensual heat in his gaze made her toes curl in her Jimmy Choos. He'd changed into a pair of fitted jeans and pale blue knit shirt, and it didn't escape her notice that he was wearing the tie she'd given him, which not only looked ridiculous with his informal outfit, but it also added to her confusion as to why he was there.

When she continued to stare at him, he tipped his head and offered her a friendly smile. "Can I come in?"

Amanda's curiosity prompted her to step back so he could enter her apartment. "Sure."

He walked past her and into her living room, and she followed behind with a resounding *click, click, click* of her heels on the floor, which made her acutely aware of how equally ridiculous *she* looked in her pajamas and heels.

He took in her upscale Manhattan apartment and contemporary furnishings, then turned back around to look at her. "Nice place."

"Thanks." Unable to bear a string of polite chit-chat, she decided to get right down to business. "Christian…what are you doing here?"

He casually slid his hands into the front pockets of his jeans, but his expression reflected something far more direct and purposeful. "I'm wearing the tie you gave me."

"I see that." The big question in her mind was *why* was he wearing the tie? To tease and torment her, no doubt. "I'm glad you like it."

"I do like it," he said, his voice dropping to a husky pitch as he stroked the strip of fabric with his fingers in a too-seductive caress. "Very much."

She swallowed hard, unsure of where this conversation was heading. She wasn't about to assume anything at this point. "And you're here because…?"

A slow, bad-boy smile kicked up the corner of his mouth as he stepped toward her, closing the distance between them. "I came here tonight to collect the other part of my Secret Santa present."

An electrifying jolt of awareness surged through Amanda, making her feel jittery. Nervous. Uncertain. And good God, even hopeful. Her throat went dry, making speech impossible at the moment.

Lifting a hand, he lazily traced the thin strap of her camisole top, down to the low scoop neck, and she bit her bottom lip to hold in a soft gasp. As he watched, her nipples tightened into hard knots against the cotton material, telling him without words how much she wanted him.

He raised his gaze back up to hers, satisfaction and a deeper, darker desire glimmering in the sapphire depths. "I believe the note you gave me with the present said something about being your lover and using the gift to tie me up so you could do all the things you've fantasized about doing to me. *That's* what I'm here for, Amanda."

Desiree chose that moment to make an appearance on her left shoulder. *Wow, he certainly has a way with words, doesn't he?*

Oh, yes, he most definitely did. Amanda was already unraveling inside, her body softening, growing warm and damp in feminine places. Still, that cautious, insecure part of her personality wanted to be sure he wasn't just toying with her. "Are you serious?"

In response, he placed his hands on her hips and moved even closer, forcing her back a few steps until her shoulders came into contact with the wall and his lower body pinned her there, as well. The unmistakable length of his erection pressed against her lower belly, which started another chain reaction of carnal desire to ripple through her.

Their faces were mere inches apart, so close that they shared each breath they took. "Now that you know my answer, how serious were you about the note you wrote to go with the tie?" he murmured. "Or was it all a joke, like you said?"

The air between them was thick and ripe with awareness, and her heart pounded an erratic rhythm in her chest. "No, it wasn't a joke," she whispered.

Lifting his hand, he slid his fingers along the side of her neck and used his thumb to tip her face up higher. His gaze searched hers with an unnerving amount of scrutiny. "Why did you write the note, Amanda?"

She'd never expected to have to explain herself or her motives behind the sexy note, and answering his question meant baring a part of her soul, which was something she'd never done with another man. In the past, she'd had physical relationships with the men she'd dated, but the emotional component had always been missing. That visceral connection that went beyond the sexual attraction or the appeal of her last name and everything that came with it.

Despite his reputation as a playboy, she felt that deeper level of intimacy with Christian and refused to spoil the moment by questioning why. There was something about him that made her feel secure, and ultimately, she trusted him with her secrets.

"I wrote you that note because I've always been attracted to you," she admitted, and looked deep into his eyes before finishing. "I wanted to do something bold and sexy that would get your attention."

"You didn't need the note or tie for that," he said as he tenderly caressed the line of her jaw with his thumb, while his other hand slipped beneath the hem of her top and his fingers brushed along the curve of her waist. "I've *always* noticed you."

She attempted to laugh, certain he was flirting with her, or trying to make her feel good. And she had to admit that the hand stroking her bare skin felt very, very good indeed. "I'm hardly your type," she pointed out, just to keep things in perspective.

"I know. And that's why I'm so attracted to you *now.*" A crooked smile canted the corners of his mouth, right before he lowered his head and gently rubbed his cheek against hers. "I can't get you, or your note, out of my head," he whispered raggedly into her ear, the defeat in his voice unmistakable. "I want you so badly, Amanda, that I can't think straight anymore."

She closed her eyes and bit her bottom lip to hold in a moan as he touched his mouth to her neck. Despite the tingling sensation unfurling deep in her belly, she thought about how he'd left her high and dry at the office earlier, and his reasons for doing so. Knowing she wouldn't be able to bear being rejected by him a second time, she had to ask, "What about regrets?"

He lifted his head from hers and both of his hands came up to cradle her face in his palms. She opened her eyes, stared into his, and saw nothing but hunger and pure carnal heat. For *her.* Her pulse quickened and she suddenly felt breathless.

"No regrets. I swear." A sinful grin transformed his features, and with a roll of his hips he branded her with the heat and impressive length of his erection confined behind the zipper of his jeans. "Just a whole lot of mutual pleasure. I promise this weekend will stay just between the two of us. But ultimately, it's up to you."

He wasn't offering her any kind of promises, but she knew better than to expect anything beyond this moment from a carefree guy like Christian. This was all about sating long-denied desires between the two of them, nothing more. And after so many years of being a good girl and a dutiful, virtuous daughter, she was ready to break free of those restraints and enjoy this one night with him, guilt-free.

She smoothed her palm down the tie he was still wearing, excited by the thought of fulfilling her fantasy with him. "Yes," she whispered, and sighed when he dropped his mouth to hers and surprised her with a deep kiss infused with lust and an exciting amount of aggression. A demanding kiss that left no doubt in her mind how badly he wanted her.

Oh, yeah, Desiree cheered gleefully. *We are so getting lucky tonight, and it's about damn time!*

Amanda couldn't help but feel the same way.

After a while, Christian gentled the kiss. "God, you taste good," he murmured against her lips. "I just want to eat you up."

The image of him doing something so wicked caused a surge of heat to settle in her stomach like fine cognac, making her feel dizzy and drunk on this man's brand of seduction. "It's Ben & Jerry's chocolate fudge brownie," she felt compelled to say.

He chuckled, then shook his head. "No, I'm absolutely certain the taste is all you," he said and resumed the kiss, stealing her breath and what little was left of her sanity.

His hands left her face and moved to her neck, then lower, gliding across her shoulders until his fingers hooked into the straps of her camisole. He dragged the thin straps down both of her arms, to her elbows, effectively causing the front of her top to follow in the same direction. Cool air rushed across her bared skin, making her shiver. Instantly, a large, warm palm cupped one of her breasts, and he gently squeezed the plump flesh as his thumb rasped over the hard, aching tip. Her sensitive nipple stiffened even more, and his appreciative male groan vibrated against their still-fused lips.

She moved restlessly against Christian, rubbing her hips against his in search of a more intimate touch. As if sensing exactly what she craved, he skimmed his free hand along the curve of her waist, then tugged the waistband of her pajama bottoms lower, until he was able to easily slip his hand inside her pants. His long fingers stroked her lower belly, traced the elastic band of her panties down to the apex of her thighs, then finally, *finally,* dipped beneath the damp silk fabric of her panties.

He wrenched his mouth from hers, buried his face against her neck and growled deep in his throat, the sound raw and primal. "God," he breathed. "You are so soft here. So hot and wet."

Those erotic words made her melt even more.

His touch was delicate at first, teasing her with soft, feathery caresses that only built her need and anticipation for more. Then he pushed deeper inside her, filling her exactly where she needed to be filled, and stroking her with his thumb exactly where she needed to be stroked. And if his expert caresses weren't enough to send her spinning out of control, he lowered his head and took one of her breasts in his mouth, his tongue licking and swirling over her tight nipple.

She sucked in a quick breath as everything within her clamored for the release he was coaxing from her. She was so aroused, so ready to indulge in the sensual pleasure he was creating with his mouth and fingers. Closing her eyes, she threaded her fingers through his hair, clenched the soft strands in her fist. She let her head fall back against the wall, and knew she was about to surrender her body, maybe even a piece of her heart and soul, to Christian.

Once you cross that line, there will be no going back to the simple, uncomplicated way it was between the two of you. Are you sure that's what you want?

Jarred out of the sensual fog consuming her, Amanda's eyes blinked open, and she prayed that she hadn't just heard Angie's prim and proper voice in her head. Not now, when her decision about Christian and making love with him was already made.

Shhhh! This forceful hush came from Desiree, confirming that the duo had reappeared to wreak havoc with Amanda's conscience. *You're so killing the moment for Amanda.*

Angie's chin lifted determinedly. *Well, someone has to think sensibly before—*

Heaven forbid, she has an orgasm? Desiree cut in, her sarcasm unmistakable. *She's so due, you know!*

The feel of Christian's mouth on her breast, and his fingers working the best kind of magic elsewhere clashed with the bickering, distracting voices in her head. Finally, Amanda just couldn't take it anymore.

"Oh, stop already!" she muttered firmly. *"Please!"*

Everything went silent and still. Including Christian. His hot, heavy breathing wafted across the dampness on her breast, and the fingers inside her, along with the pressure and friction of his thumb against her clitoris, immediately stopped.

Oh, God. She couldn't believe that she'd actually spoken out loud. She waited for Christian's reaction to the words she'd accidentally blurted out in frustration. Slowly, he lifted his head and looked into her eyes, searching deeply. His own gaze was a dark, smoldering shade of blue, and a concerned frown creased his brows.

"You want me to stop?" he asked gruffly, and judging by the tense set of his muscles, she knew he'd bring the encounter to a halt if that was what she really, truly wanted.

But, the last thing she wanted him to do was stop, and was certain she'd die if he didn't finish what he'd started. She'd been so, so close, and it wasn't going to take much more to send her soaring over that edge of release.

"No, I didn't mean you," she said and inwardly cringed at the way that sounded, as well as the confusion etching his features. Knowing there were no words to explain what had just happened that didn't make her seem like a crazy woman, she grabbed the tie hanging from around his neck and tugged his head back down to her breasts.

And just in case there were any last doubts or concerns lingering in his mind, she brazenly whispered her desires in his ear. "Make me come, Christian. Please."

With a ragged groan, he picked up where he'd abruptly left off as if he'd never stopped. His teeth grazed her nipple, followed by a soothing lap of his tongue, and between her thighs, his hand and fingers moved in a slow, provocative rhythm designed to heighten the tension pulling tighter and tighter within her.

Ahhh, that's much better, Desiree sighed.

Go away! Refusing to let Desiree and Angie be voyeurs and ruin what was going to possibly be the best sex of her life, Amanda banished them completely from her mind. With the two of them gone, her sole focus became Christian, and her own shameless desires.

The man was a master, and when he'd teased her to the point of exquisite torture, he finally gave her body what it ultimately needed. A slick, deliberate stroke along her flesh. A slow, deep thrust of his fingers. The suction of his mouth on her breast that seemed to spiral all the way down to her sex, then snapped free in a burst of sensation.

The orgasm that swept through her was pure, unadulterated ecstasy, like a full-body climax, touching on every erogenous zone she possessed, and some she didn't even know existed. Her toes curled in her Jimmy Choos, her blood rushed to her head in a dizzying surge, and she cried out and shuddered against the pulsing sensation buffeting her entire body.

When the incredible pleasure finally ebbed and she came to her senses moments later, Christian was kissing and nuzzling her neck, his breath hot and damp on her skin. He eased his hand out of her pajama pants and lifted the straps of her camisole back up to her shoulders, covering her tender, swollen breasts.

Confusion trickled through her, clearing the passionate fog from her mind. He couldn't be done—he was still hard as a rock and she was ready and willing to give him just as much sensual satisfaction.

"Christian?" Tangling her fingers in the hair at the nape of his neck, she gently tugged his head back so she could look at his face and search his gaze. "What about you?"

"God, I want you, Amanda," he said, the heat and unquenched lust in his darkened eyes backing his claim. "I want to know the sexy, uninhibited woman who wrote me such a provocative note and promised to tie me up and have her way with me. All you have to do is say yes if you want this to go any further."

Emboldened by the strength of her desire for him, and eager to be the bold, brazen woman Christian wanted, her answer didn't require a whole lot of thought.

"Yes," she said, and taking his hand in hers, she led him back to her bedroom.

Chapter Four

As Amanda switched on the lamp on the nightstand, Christian took a quick glance around her spacious master bedroom. He smiled to himself, thinking the furnishings and decor reflected just how soft and feminine Amanda was beneath that no-nonsense facade she presented at work.

He liked what he saw. A whole lot. A cream-and-lavender floral comforter and ruffled pillows covered her mattress, and matching curtains framed the windows. The bed frame was a rich antique iron, with bars and scroll accents. The wallpaper in the room was textured, and the dresser and armoire were white-washed and elegant in design.

As he continued to scan the room, a framed picture on the wall of a man, woman and child caught his attention. It was an older photograph, depicting a much younger version of Douglas Creighton, a woman he assumed was Amanda's mother and a little girl of about ten who possessed the same features as the beautiful woman Amanda had become. It was a family portrait, obviously taken long ago, and it made him realize how little he really knew about Amanda outside the office, other than the fact that she was an only child.

He wanted to know more. About her family. Her past. Her childhood. And even what she saw for herself when she contemplated her future. That notion startled him, considering how intimate and personal his own thoughts had become when it came to Amanda. It also made him realize how deeply he was into her, despite all the potential complications of getting involved with the boss's daughter. Yet, even knowing what was at stake, he couldn't bring himself to turn around and walk away from her, and this night together.

Then his troubling thoughts scattered as she strolled back toward him, a sultry smile on her lips, her gaze bright with seductive intent. He was helpless to resist this sweet, sexy woman who'd sent him such a tantalizing Secret Santa gift. A woman who clearly wanted him as much as he ached for her.

Stopping in front of him, she reached for his tie and pulled it free of its knot. "I'm going to be needing this in just a few minutes," she murmured huskily and tossed the long scrap of material onto the bed behind him for safekeeping. Then she tugged the hem of his shirt from his pants and pulled it over his head and off.

She ran her hands over his chest, sighing appreciatively as she slowly skimmed her palms downward, touching and caressing her way to the waistband of his jeans. But before she could reach the snap securing his pants, he playfully pushed her hands aside, knowing one firm stroke of her fingers could easily set him off, and that would be the end for him.

"Not just yet," he said and hooked his own fingers into her pajama bottoms. He pushed them down, over the curve of her hips, along her slender thighs, then let the soft cotton pants drop to her ankles.

She tried to step out of the bottoms, but the material got caught around her feet and she laughed a bit self-consciously. "I need to take off my shoes."

The last thing he wanted was her removing those high heels she was wearing. At least not yet. "I'll help you out." Crouching down, he gently eased one foot, then the other, out of the pants while she held on to his shoulders for balance.

Slowly, he stood back up, trailing his fingers along her legs, her hips, her waist, as he took in the entire length of Amanda's gorgeous body. Finally, he straightened to his full height, as did his cock. There was something so damned erotic about Amanda Creighton standing in front of him, her hair tousled around her face and wearing nothing more than a skimpy camisole top, silky panties and bright red four-inch heels. He'd noticed those shoes earlier, mainly because they were the exact opposite of the prim, conservative pumps she always wore at the office.

She shifted on her feet and bit her bottom lip. "Umm, you forgot to take off my shoes while you were down there."

He grinned rakishly, thinking of a few other wicked things he could have done while he'd been kneeling in front of her. "Be patient, sweetheart. I'm getting there." Sitting down on the bed, he patted the mattress between his spread legs. "Put your foot up here for me and I'll take care of those shoes for you."

Doing as he asked, she lifted her leg and braced her foot right where he indicated. Her toenails were painted a daring red, he noticed, as he slipped a thin strip of leather through the tiny buckle wrapped around her ankle.

"So, what's with wearing the dress-up shoes with your pajamas?" he asked, glancing up at her face as he took that high heel off and started in on the other.

A warm flush of color rose in her cheeks, probably because she was just as aware of the fact that she'd never worn such provocative shoes to work before. "I just bought them and I was trying them on to see how they fit when you arrived."

"Well, I like them." He unfastened the second strap and let the shoe drop to the floor, but kept his fingers circled around her ankle to keep her foot in place on the bed between his thighs. "They make your legs look longer and sexier than they already are." To prove his point, he slowly, leisurely skimmed his fingers over her calf, behind her knee and along the inside of her smooth, silky thighs.

Her skin quivered beneath the stroke of his fingers, and her nipples tightened against her cotton top. Loving her reaction to his touch, and wanting a more physical contact with her, he put her foot back to the floor and stood up. Then he wrapped an arm around her back and brought her body flush to his, from her soft breasts all the way down to her supple thighs.

She felt incredible in his arms. Incredibly *perfect.* More so than any woman he'd ever been with.

His hand wandered downward, following the slope of her spine and over the sweet curve of her ass. He squeezed her bottom, and wished he'd gotten rid of her panties when he'd had the chance. "Do you know what men call shoes like the ones you were wearing?"

Placing her hands on his bare chest, she smiled up at him with an innocent bat of her lashes. "Dress-up shoes?" she replied cheekily.

He chuckled, then dipped his head close to hers and whispered his scandalous answer in her ear. "No, they call them 'fuck me' shoes, because that's what it makes a man think of when he sees a woman wearing them. And that's exactly what I want to do to you."

His intent made her shiver, and she laughed softly against his cheek. "Tonight, it's going to be the other way around."

He groaned, this assertive side to Amanda heightening his excitement, along with the need to be inside of her. Soon. "Lucky me."

She leaned back, her eyes sparkling with desire. "Well, I do need to make good on the Secret Santa gift I gave to you, now don't I?"

"Oh, yeah," he growled. Letting her go for a moment, he reached into the front pocket of his jeans and pulled out half a dozen foil packets. "I came prepared." He grinned sheepishly.

An amused smile curved her lips. "And you're obviously very confident and feeling quite ambitious, considering how many condoms you brought."

He shrugged unrepentantly. "Hey, a guy can hope."

She took the packets from him and tossed them onto the pillow with the blue-and-gray striped tie. Then she pushed him back until he was sitting on the bed again. "Move up toward the headboard," she said, and he did as she ordered.

Settled in the middle of the bed, precisely where

Amanda wanted him, he watched her kneel on the mattress by his feet. She removed his shoes and socks, then crawled her way upward, between his spread legs, and went to work on the button and zipper on his pants. She caressed and squeezed him through the denim, making good on her promise to tease him to distraction before finally skinning his jeans and briefs down his legs and off.

He was stripped bare. She stared at his thick, aching erection and licked her lips. He imagined her mouth on him, sucking him deep, and his cock twitched and strained for any kind of attention she was willing to give. Unfortunately, she bypassed his hard-on and instead crawled up the length of his body until she was sitting astride his chest—so close that the scent of her arousal made his head spin. He was tempted to grab her thighs and pull her up higher, so he could taste her with his mouth and tongue and make her come again.

Frustrated that she was still wearing her top and panties while he wasn't wearing a stitch of clothing, he raised his gaze from the crux of her thighs, all the way up to her face. "You know, I'm feeling at a distinct disadvantage being completely naked, while you're still dressed."

"Semi-dressed," she corrected him, and reached for the tie on the pillow beside his head. "Besides, you had your chance to get me naked. But don't worry, I'll get there, too."

"I seriously can't wait." His stomach tightened as she wove the strip of silk between her fingers in a slow, erotic show of seduction and possession. Sitting on his chest with that *I'm-so-going-to-do-you* look in her eyes, she was his every fantasy come to life.

She leaned over the upper half of his body to secure his wrists together, then fastened them to one of the iron rods with a firm, inescapable knot. Her breasts were literally in his face and he nuzzled the soft, lush weight before turning his head and gently biting one of her nipples through the cotton T.

She gasped in shock and sat up straight, then narrowed her gaze playfully. "You are *so* going to pay for that."

"God, I hope so." He grinned.

She grabbed one of the condoms, but instead of getting right to business, she scooted her bottom down a bit, until his erection met the damp barrier of her panties. Face-to-face now, she lowered her mouth to his and kissed him—a slow, hot, deep kiss that made him hungry for so much more. Her damp lips traveled leisurely to his neck, down his throat, to his chest. Her soft hands followed, caressing and stroking his skin, and he groaned when her tongue flicked over one taut nipple, then sucked in a quick breath when her teeth scraped across the sensitive tip.

He felt her smile against his chest that she'd gotten even with her own love bite, then that incredible mouth and wet tongue of hers was forging a path of erotic pleasure down his stomach, until she was kneeling between his legs.

At the first delicate touch of her tongue on the tip of his cock, his entire body shuddered and his hands clenched around the bonds securing his arms to the headboard. Her lips parted over the head, and he growled deep in his throat as she took his entire shaft into her warm, wet mouth and stroked him deep. The silky strands of her hair brushed across his thighs, adding to the sensual sensations, and just when the tension inside of him started to spiral toward the breaking point, she pulled away and tore open the foil packet.

He realized he was panting for breath, and he hadn't even come yet. He glanced down toward the foot of the bed, watching as Amanda rolled the condom on him, using both hands to do it, her own erratic breathing reflecting just how excited and eager she was, as well.

Once she had him sheathed, she sat back and peeled off her top, her full, lush breasts bouncing gently now that they were unbound. Then she shimmied out of her panties and tossed them aside.

Gloriously, beautifully naked, she straddled his hips, took his cock in her hand, and eased him inside of her. She slowly, gradually lowered herself, prolonging the moment, until he found himself deep, deep inside her.

Splaying her palms on his lower belly, she raised her heavy-lidded gaze to his, her mouth lifting in a purely female smile as she set out to drive him crazy with need. She moved her hips in small circles that eventually gave way to sexier, more uninhibited strokes that increased the pleasure and friction between them. And with each breath-stealing glide of her body against his, he slid deeper, and grew impossibly harder, inside her.

He automatically tried to reach down to caress her breasts, her belly and thighs, but the ties on his wrists reminded him that he was a slave to her desires. God, he wanted to touch her in the worst way, and he would, *next* time. And there was no doubt in his mind that they *would* make love again, because he was coming to realize that having her once wasn't going to be nearly enough for him. He wanted more...more of Amanda and everything that made her the incredible woman she was.

It didn't take him long to realize that he didn't need to touch Amanda at all. She knew exactly what she wanted from him, what moves aroused her the most, and she didn't hesitate to do whatever felt good.

That in itself was a huge turn-on for him, and as her climax escalated toward that ultimate sexual bliss, so did his own.

With a soft, ragged moan, she dropped her head back and arched into him, shamelessly grinding against his groin as her orgasm rippled through her. Her inner contractions milked his shaft, and the tight, slick grip unraveled the last of his restraint in a hot and potent release that wrung him dry and ripped a strangled cry from his throat.

She collapsed on top of him and buried her face against his neck, her breathing warm and damp against his skin. She sighed softly, languidly, and he had the thought that this woman knew exactly how to tease him, please him and make him lose control, just as her note had suggested.

He smiled to himself. This night with her was, by far, the best Secret Santa gift anyone had ever given him.

Christian turned onto his side and reached his arm across the bed, but the warm, soft female body he'd slept with, and made love with the entire night, was gone. He came awake slowly, the scent of Amanda and sex filling every breath he inhaled. It was a great way to wake up, and that's all it took to rouse his senses, and other parts of his anatomy.

A sleepy glance at the clock on the nightstand told him it was 8:24 in the morning on Saturday, and his completely sated body confirmed that last night hadn't been a dream, but a vivid, provocative reality. One that had sent his life as he knew it spinning in a direction he never would have anticipated.

He rolled to his back and stretched, a smile easing up the corners of his mouth as erotic memories flooded his mind. Who would have thought that cool, poised Amanda Creighton was such a temptress in private? Who would have thought that Amanda Creighton would become the one woman he wanted more than just a casual fling with?

Startling, but true. Sure, he'd always been attracted to her, and while sex with Amanda had been phenomenal, there were so many other things about her that intrigued him, so many contradictions that made him curious to know her on a deeper, more emotional level. It wasn't a smart move, all things considered. Like the fact that she was the boss's daughter. Like the fact that he'd worked damn hard to get that coveted promotion that Doug Creighton had the ability to give, or take away.

Still, knowing all that, he wasn't quite ready to end things with Amanda. And with that thought in mind, he hauled himself out of bed so they could make the most of their day together. That was, if she didn't already have plans.

He heard noises from another part of the apartment, and judging by the clattering sounds, he guessed she was in the kitchen. Perfect. With her busy, it gave him time to take a quick shower before greeting her. As he crossed the room, he glanced at an open door and realized it was her closet. A *huge* walk-in closet, and he switched on the light, curious to see what was inside.

Lots of clothes, obviously, and he couldn't help but grin at the way they were all hung up in a neat, orderly fashion by pants, blouses, dresses, then sorted by color. There were drawers and cubbyholes filled with purses and belts and those sensible shoes she wore to work, but what drew his attention was the custom-built, floor-to-ceiling rack displaying dozens of colorful, sexy, high-heel shoes. The strappy, traffic-stopping kind she'd worn last night with her pajamas.

"Well, I'll be damned," he murmured in amusement. It appeared that Ms. Creighton had a shoe fetish of some sort. One she kept private for some reason, because he sure as hell hadn't seen her wearing any of those hot, seductive shoes before. And they were just too provocative for any man not to sit up and take notice if they had been on her feet.

This secret side to Amanda was yet another intriguing facet to her personality.

He continued on to the bathroom and noticed that she'd left a brand new toothbrush on the counter for him, which he appreciated. He took a quick hot shower and got dressed, sans the tie this morning. After finger-combing his damp hair, he strolled barefoot down the hall, following the scent of coffee and something else that smelled delicious, according to his rumbling, empty stomach.

He stopped at the entryway into the kitchen, where Amanda was standing at the stove cooking breakfast. Choosing just to watch her for a few minutes without making his arrival known, he leaned against the doorjamb and took in the long-sleeve pink sweater she was wearing and the crisp, new-looking pair of designer jeans that hugged her curves, including that fine ass of hers that he'd held in his hands more than once last night. Much to his disappointment, on her feet were practical leather loafers, instead of one of those pairs of sexy, flirtatious shoes in her closet.

He was going to have to do something to change that.

He heard her say something, and thinking she was talking to him, he lifted his gaze from her feet back up—and realized that she was still facing away from him as she buttered some toast, still unaware of his presence. She was carrying on a one-way conversation with herself, and it wasn't the first time he'd caught her doing so. There was that time in the break room yesterday, and again last night when he could have sworn she'd asked him to stop touching her and she'd tried to explain it away with a strange "no, not you" remark.

"Yeah, yeah, yeah," Amanda said with a sigh. "I have to admit it was pretty damn good. The best sex I've ever had."

He grinned. Male ego aside, Christian liked the fact that he'd given her something no man ever had before, and knew he felt the same way about her. "Me, too."

She abruptly whirled around, a butter knife in her hand and her eyes wide with surprise. "I didn't know you were out of the shower already."

Pushing off the doorjamb, he strolled across the kitchen toward her. "It would have taken much longer, and been far more enjoyable, if you would have joined me." She blushed, and he kissed her soft, parted lips, lingering just long enough to let her know that last night meant something more to him than a one-night stand. "Good morning."

"Morning," she replied huskily, and absently licked her bottom lip before turning back to her task. "Would you like some coffee?"

"Sure, I'll get it." There was already a second mug on the counter for him, and he poured himself a cup before glancing at the two plates of food on the counter. "Breakfast smells terrific."

"Good." She cut two slices of toast in half and added them to their dishes. "I made you a vegetable-and-cheese omelet. I hope that's okay."

"It's certainly better than the bowl of Cheerios I usually eat in the morning, and it's very appreciated. I'm starved." Picking up his mug of coffee, he took a sip as she carried their breakfast to the small kitchen table. "So, do you talk to yourself often?" he asked.

She stiffened ever so slightly, seemed to regain her composure, then turned toward him again. She shrugged, but surprisingly didn't deny her penchant for personal conversations. "It's an odd habit of mine," she said, waving dismissively as she went to the refrigerator and pulled out a pitcher of orange juice.

Odd, yes, but also endearing. And since it was clear that the topic embarrassed her, he switched to a different, but equally intriguing, one. "I do have a curious question for you."

She poured two glasses of OJ and cast him a cautious, uncertain glance. "Okay."

"You know those shoes you wore last night?"

She looked away, but not before he saw yet another flush of pink sweep across her cheeks, as if she were remembering what he'd said about those high heels he'd taken off for her. "Yes."

"Well, I couldn't help but notice that you have a whole closet full of them." She lifted a brow as if to ask what he'd been doing in her closet, but he wasn't about to let her sidetrack this conversation, too. "How come you never wear any of those shoes to work?"

"Because they aren't appropriate for the office," she said and set the two glasses of orange juice on the table.

Her answer came much too easily, as if she'd spent years convincing herself of that fact. What she didn't realize, however, was that he'd seen that quick glimpse of insecurity in her gaze before she'd masked it with a nonchalant reply.

He tipped his head, daring to challenge her. "Says who?"

"It's not exactly the image I want to portray at work," she tried to explain, but he sensed her reasons ran much deeper than that. "Besides, it's more of a hobby for me than anything else."

"Collecting designer shoes?" he asked incredulously.

She came up beside him and topped off her own mug with the steaming coffee. "Hey, we all have our quirks."

Hers were just a bit more eccentric than most. Who spent hundreds of dollars on shoes that they didn't wear and enjoy? "You really ought to put them to good use and wear them." He reached out and brushed the backs of his fingers across her smooth cheek. Her gaze softened, and something very near to the vicinity of his heart gave a distinct *thump* of emotional awareness. "Those shoes change the way you look, the way you carry yourself. They make you look damn sexy and very confident."

Laughing lightly, she flitted away from him and headed to the table with her mug in hand. "Well, I'm sure I'd shock everyone, including my father, if I came strutting into work in four-inch strappy heels."

Ahhh, her father. He wondered at their relationship outside of the office, if he'd been a strict parent with her, or if being so reserved was all her own doing. "Maybe the first day, yes," he agreed as he sat down next to her. "But honestly, who cares? Why not wear them because they make *you* feel good?"

She picked up her fork and smiled at him. "I *do* wear them."

"In private. At home." He grinned wryly. "Wow, you're such a rebel."

She wrinkled her nose at him, but didn't reply to his comment, choosing instead to let the entire subject slide, which she was very good at, he was coming to realize.

"So, what are you doing for the holidays?" she asked brightly.

His stomach growled hungrily, and he dug into his omelet. "I'm driving to my parents' house in Boston tomorrow afternoon."

"You're not flying?" she asked, surprised.

He shook his head. "It's only a three-hour drive and I do it all the time. My whole family will be there tomorrow for Christmas eve, and then stay until Christmas morning to open presents. It's a yearly tradition. What about you?"

She ate a bite of her breakfast and chased it down with a drink of orange juice. "I'll be spending Christmas with my father and his wife and a few of their friends. Nothing too exciting."

Her father's *wife*. So, Douglas Creighton had remarried at some point. "And your mother? Do you get to spend time with her?"

She wiped her mouth with her napkin, a bit of sadness coloring her eyes. "Actually, she died a long time ago."

"I'm sorry to hear that." He placed his hand over hers on the table and gave it a gentle squeeze. "Is she the woman in the picture hanging on the wall in your room?"

At the mention of the portrait, her gaze warmed again. "You noticed that?"

He was beginning to notice everything about her. "Yes, but only for a quick moment before you distracted me for the rest of the night." He winked at her.

She laughed at his playful comment, just as he'd intended. "Yeah, that's my mom," she said, tucking a stray strand of silky hair behind her ear. "It's been a long time since she passed away. I was only twelve when she died, and there are times I really do miss her. Especially around the holidays."

He could only imagine how difficult this time of year was for her, considering both of his parents were still alive and he had enough siblings to turn the holidays into one big party. Suddenly, he didn't want her spending the weekend alone when she could be spending it with him. At least until he had to leave for Boston.

Finished with his breakfast, he pushed his plate aside. "Hey, what are you doing today?"

She thought for a moment. "Not much."

So far, so good. "Any last-minute Christmas shopping you have to do?"

"Not really. I'm done. Everything is bought and wrapped."

"Why am I not surprised?" he teased, certain she'd finished her Christmas shopping a month ago. "As for me, I'm one of those last-minute holiday shoppers, and I sure could use some help picking out gifts for my sisters and nieces. Care to join me?"

She stared at him as if he were insane. "Are you

crazy? It's less than two days before Christmas. Isn't it a madhouse at every store out there today?"

"Of course it is." He grinned persuasively. "You just haven't fully experienced the spirit of Christmas until you've been in the midst of holiday shopping twenty-four hours before Christmas eve."

"Okay, you are crazy," she said and laughed, her eyes sparkling merrily. "But what the hell. I'm game."

"Good." Now came the good part—a little nudge from him for her to embrace that sensual woman he'd been with last night. "*But,* there is one condition if you want to join me."

Her gaze narrowed with amused suspicion. "And what kind of condition would that be?"

He took a long drink of his coffee, drawing out the moment and letting her imagination take flight before he said, "I want you to wear one of those pairs of designer shoes in your closet."

"You've got to be joking." She sat back in her chair and shook her head. "In case you haven't noticed, it's winter in New York and it's freezing outside."

There was no way he was going to let Amanda talk her way out of this one. "I saw a few pairs of sexy high-heeled boots among all those opened-toed shoes, and I'm sure any one of them would keep your feet warm and toasty." He leaned closer, and before she could go on about practicality, he tossed out a little challenge he was certain she wouldn't be able to resist. "Unless, of course, you're afraid of getting them scuffed."

She opened her mouth, then closed it again, clamping her lips together. After a moment, she let loose a soft peal of laughter. "You are so—"

"Irresistible?" he offered.

"Actually, I was thinking more along the lines of *manipulative,*" she grumbled good-naturedly.

He took the playful insult in stride. "Hey, whatever it takes to make you live a little on the wild side, sweetheart."

She sighed in exasperation, which contradicted the smile threatening to spill across her lips. "Okay. Fine. You win."

He grinned triumphantly. "Yeah, I usually do."

Chapter Five

After a long, extremely fun day of hitting most of the big department stores in Manhattan, and being a part of the Christmas craze, Amanda was exhausted. Christian, with his last-minute gift-buying energy, gave the expression *shop till you drop* new meaning. But, Amanda had to admit that she'd had a great time and enjoyed assisting Christian in picking out gifts for the females in his family.

Once he'd crossed the last person off his gift list, he'd taken her to dinner for Italian fare at Puttanesca. Feeling very mellow after consuming two glasses of wine over the course of their meal, he'd taken advantage of that fact by cajoling her into coming back to his place to help him wrap the dozens of toys and gifts he'd purchased. Not that she would have refused him under any circumstances, but she didn't want to appear easy and preferred to make him work for her assent.

Now, they were sitting cross-legged and barefoot

in the middle of his living room, with the coffee table pushed out of the way to give them room to spread out. The floor was littered with tape, scissors, rolls and rolls of Christmas wrapping paper, and dozens of bright, colorful ribbon and stick-on bows. After Christian had sheepishly confessed his lack of talent when it came to wrapping packages—and confirmed it as well when his first attempt looked as though a five-year-old had done the job—they decided that he'd stick to the kid's presents and she'd take care of the adults. Their system had worked very well, and two hours later they were nearly done with the huge pile of gifts.

Finished wrapping his mother's crystal tapered candlestick holders, Amanda pulled a long stream of ribbon from the roll and went to work giving the package a pretty finishing touch. She glanced at Christian and hid a smile as she watched the intense way he was concentrating on attempting to fold the wrapping paper around an oddly shaped box that held a Tonka truck for one of his nephews. He came up short on one end and let out a growl of frustration that made her laugh.

"I'm so glad I'm able to amuse you," he said wryly.

She curled the hunter-green ribbon on the present with the sharp end of her scissors and added a name tag. "You know, it's really not that difficult if you just take your time and make sure you fold the ends a little more neatly."

He rolled his eyes humorously as he taped a strip of wrapping paper where he'd fallen short, giving the package a patchwork look. "I'm not putting that kind of effort into the kids' presents. They're going to rip into them without even noticing the wrapping job."

"That's why you're in charge of their gifts, and I'm doing the grown-ups." She set his mother's present with the rest that she'd wrapped, and grinned as she noticed the big difference between her pile of lavishly decorated gifts and his stack of haphazardly wrapped packages. "Do you think they'll be able to tell you had help?"

"Definitely." He returned her grin with one of his own. "Yours are way too fancy. But they look great. Thank you." He leaned over and showed his gratitude with a warm, soft kiss on her lips.

Such a simple touch between them, but it was enough to start a slow burn of desire for him. "It was my pleasure," she murmured when he finally pulled away. And truly, it was. She only had a few gifts to wrap each year, and she loved the whole relaxing, creative process of choosing just the right holiday paper, ribbon and bows to embellish a present.

"You certainly have a huge family," she said, taking in all the gifts they'd bought and wrapped—all in one day, no less. While they'd been shopping earlier, then at dinner, he'd regaled her with tales about his siblings—two older sisters and a younger brother—along with a small passel of nieces and nephews he seemed to absolutely adore. "It must be crazy on Christmas Day."

He topped off the Tonka truck with a pre-made, stick-on bow, and added a name tag with his nephew's name on it. "Yeah, it's loud and boisterous and a whole lot of fun."

She could only imagine, and could easily see Christian on the floor playing with his nieces and nephews. As an only child, she'd never have those experiences, and envied him that. "You're very lucky to have a big family."

"Try telling me that when I was a teenager and fighting my two sisters and brother for the bathroom in the morning before school," he griped, but there was a sincere fondness for his siblings in his gaze.

"At least you had siblings. It was very, very quiet in my house." And incredibly lonely at times, too, which always gave Desiree and Angie the opportunity to keep her company.

Christian rummaged through one of the bags from a department store and pulled out a silver box with a matching satin silver ribbon tied around it. "Hey, look what I found," he said in mock surprise. "One last gift."

She eyed the box, trying to remember when and where he'd bought that particular present, but her mind came up blank. "Luckily for you, it's already wrapped. And very elegantly, I might add. How did you manage that?" she teased.

"I can't claim responsibility for this one. I had the clerk at Sak's take care of this gift on the sly." He handed the box to her, his gaze a dark, intimate shade of blue. "It's for you."

"Me?" She was shocked, mainly because a present of any sort from Christian was the last thing she expected. For that matter, her weekend with him was all the gift she wanted, and needed. "When did you manage to buy this?"

He shrugged. "When you were picking out a perfume set for my sister."

Ahh, now she remembered. He'd asked her to choose what fragrance she thought one of his sisters might like, while he'd ventured over to women's accessories, which was where she'd found him fifteen minutes later. Obviously, he'd accomplished a lot in that short span of time.

She fingered the satin ribbon, and though she was secretly pleased that he'd thought of her, she didn't want him to think a gift was necessary. "Well, you really shouldn't have."

"I wanted to. Besides, I couldn't resist. Really." He winked at her, a wicked gleam in his eyes. "Go on, open it up."

Unable to stem the excitement and curiosity rising within her, she untied the bow and pulled off the ribbon. She opened the lid, peeled away the signature tissue paper and gasped when she saw something silky in the brightest, most gorgeous jewel-toned shades she'd ever seen. There were purples, pinks, blues and greens in an abstract design, the kind of rich and vibrant colors that gave her such a rush of pleasure.

Uncertain exactly what it was, she lifted the luxurious fabric out of the box and realized that it was a silk scarf. And an expensive, high-end, Emilio Pucci one at that. The man certainly had great taste.

Stunned, knowing that the hand-picked gift had to cost him a small fortune, she swallowed hard and glanced back at Christian. He was watching her intently, waiting for her reaction, and she knew deep in her heart that there was more behind Christian's reason for giving her this gift than it just being a designer scarf.

"It's absolutely beautiful," she said, her voice raspy with emotion.

He reached out and touched the line of her jaw then smoothed his thumb down to her lips. "When I saw that scarf, it immediately reminded me of all those colorful, sexy shoes you have in your closet. You were meant to wear bold, sensual things, Amanda."

She hugged the scarf to her chest, holding it for the cherished, insightful gift it was. "I love it. Thank you." Her words felt so inadequate for what he'd given her.

She was so incredibly touched because no one had ever given her something so intimate and meaningful. It occurred to her that in just one day together he'd proven to her with this gift that he knew her better than her own father or friends did. That beneath her practical and staid clothing and personality there was a woman who ached to be confident and daring enough to wear those colorful designer shoes in her closet, and the jewel-toned scarf he'd bought for her.

And she was beginning to think that maybe, just maybe, she could be that woman after all.

Overwhelmed by the onslaught of indescribable emotions she was feeling for this man, she leaned over and *showed* him how grateful she was for everything he'd given her this weekend. More than just sex and a good time. More than just a scarf. He'd given her a sense of self and quite possibly the confidence to embrace her inner vixen. And wouldn't Desiree be pleased with that?

Her lips met his, and she kissed him with hunger, passion and a soul-deep longing that rocked her to the very core. She touched her hand to his stubbled cheek, and his fingers tangled in her hair, tipping her head just so to deepen the connection of their mouths, and the erotic swirl and slide of their tongues. The kiss quickly turned wild and hot, to the point that she was seriously contemplating tearing off his clothes and having her way with him right in the middle of all the wrapping paper and bows. But before she could follow through with that plan, it was Christian who slowed things down a bit.

"You know," he whispered against her lips as he continued to tease her with soft, damp kisses, "I have to admit when I first saw that scarf I thought about all the different ways you could use it."

"Really?" Despite feeling light-headed and breath-less, and getting hotter by the minute, she managed a smile against his mouth. "Why do I get the impression that you're not thinking about it accessorizing an outfit?"

"Maybe because I'm not." He chuckled, the low, sinful sound causing her breasts to swell and her nipples to tighten into hard, sensitive knots that ached for the touch of his fingers. The warm, wet suction of his mouth.

Remembering what she'd done to him with the tie, she pulled back so she could look into his eyes, which had grown dark and smoky with desire. "You want to tie me up with the scarf?"

"Oh, yeah," he growled sexily. "That, and a whole lot more." He stood up and held out his hand to her. "Care to find out exactly what I have in mind?"

She glanced up, unable to miss just how aroused he was, or the heat and seductive promise in his eyes. Helpless to resist this one last night with him, she stood up, too. Then she put her hand in his and let him lead her to his bedroom…and straight into temptation of the sweetest kind.

Amanda stepped out of Christian's shower, grabbed the big, fluffy towel hanging on the wall hook, and dried off, including her wet hair. Once she was done, she wrapped it around her body and tucked the end between her breasts to keep the towel secured.

She'd taken a nice, hot, relaxing shower while Christian had gone down to the corner café for coffee and pastries for breakfast, and now the bathroom was filled with fragrant steam, which made it difficult to use the mirror since it was completely fogged. She cracked open the door to let a bit of cool air in, and used a hand towel to wipe off a spot on the mirror so she could see her reflection.

She was unexpectedly greeted by Angie, who was sitting on her right shoulder, her gaze narrowed in concern as she took in Amanda's features and the warm flush of her complexion. *Oh, no, you have the look,* she said and pursed her lips in disapproval.

Amanda sighed as she picked up the wide-tooth comb on the counter and pulled it through her damp hair to the ends. She'd managed to keep the distracting duo out of her head yesterday and last night, but it appeared they were back to cause their brand of havoc with her conscience.

Of course she has the look, Desiree replied with a sly, knowing grin. *It's the glow of a woman who's enjoyed incredible, mind-blowing sex with a hot stud.*

Amanda couldn't deny the truth. "Yeah, the sex was pretty incredible, *again,*" she murmured.

If she'd thought that Friday night's pleasurable escapade and her multiple orgasms had been a fluke, then last night had confirmed that there was enough chemistry between her and Christian to set the sheets on fire. He'd used the silk scarf in ways she never would have imagined and, coupled with the fact that he was a master with his hands and mouth and fingers, Amanda had spent hours indulging in the kind of sexual bliss she'd only fantasized about before now.

No, it's more than that, Angie fretted and wrung her hands anxiously in her lap. *I'm afraid she's falling for that bad boy!*

"No, I'm not," Amanda said, but the denial lacked

any real conviction. Probably because Angie had hit too close to the truth.

Desiree leaned forward and peered intently at Amanda's features in the mirror. Her eyes widened and she abruptly sat back on Amanda's shoulder. *Uh-oh,* she said with a hint of worry in her tone. *Angie just might be right. For once.*

That comment earned Desiree a sharp glare from her nemesis, who always thought she knew best.

The comb caught on a tangle of wet hair, and Amanda gave it a forceful tug out of pure frustration—and lost a few extra strands in the process. "Well, it can't happen," she told Desiree and Angie, as well as herself.

I think it already has, Angie said in that maternal way that Amanda couldn't ignore.

Amanda frowned at her reflection. "Okay, so maybe it has," she admitted, and knew by the pounding of her heart in her chest that she had, indeed, fallen harder for Christian than she'd ever intended.

Oh, yeah, she was halfway in love with him.

She inhaled a slow, deep breath, and grabbed the counter for support as the truth of her feelings smacked her in the face. As did a good dose of reality. No matter how great their brief time together had been, she knew better than to expect anything beyond this affair. They'd both agreed upon no regrets, and

Christian had made no promises that even so much as hinted at a relationship after today.

In all honesty, this fling of theirs had all been a product of the Secret Santa note and gift she'd sent him. It had given them both permission to act on their attraction and desires and, without that bold and daring move of hers, they never would have traveled down this particular path.

So, she accepted their affair for what it was, and just hoped to God that she didn't compare every guy she dated after this weekend to Christian. Ha! Fat chance, she thought. Because despite her little pep talk, she knew deep in her heart this was a man who could have been *the one* for her.

Oh, Amanda, Angie said softly, consolingly. *I'm so sorry.*

Amanda appreciated her guardian angel's empathy, especially since Angie had been so against her involvement with Christian from the beginning. For good reasons, obviously. It appeared that Angie did know best after all. "Hey, it was a one-shot deal, and we both knew it going into this weekend."

More like five or six shots, Desiree said, using a bit of innuendo in her attempt to lighten the mood. *But really, who's counting?*

Amanda laughed and shook her head. "Obviously, *you* are."

The door behind Amanda slowly pushed open, and she glanced into the mirror to find Christian standing there, looking incredible sexy and gorgeous. He was wearing a soft gray, New York Mets pullover sweatshirt and a pair of jeans, and his thick hair was tousled around his head, as if the wind had combed his hair this morning. She had no idea when he'd returned from the café, or what, if anything, he'd overheard.

He tipped his head and grinned at her. "You talking to yourself again?"

She felt a surge of heat travel up her neck to her face, and didn't bother to try and evade his question. "Umm, guilty as charged."

He casually leaned a shoulder against the doorjamb, settling in for the moment. "You know, it really does sound as though you're talking to someone, and not just yourself." There was an abundance of curiosity in his gaze, along with something deeper that told her he suspected there was more to her one-way conversations than she was letting on.

The man was too perceptive, and she turned around to face him. "Actually, I kind of am talking to someone else." She didn't know what possessed her to make that confession to him, but once it was out, she couldn't take it back. Besides, he'd caught her muttering to herself so many times that he was probably beginning to think she was a little psychotic.

"One of those invisible, imaginary friends from childhood?" he guessed, amusement dancing in his eyes.

She'd come this far, and figured what the hell. "There are two of them, actually."

She truly expected him to burst out laughing at her elaborate tale, to tell her to stop pulling his leg, but instead he played along. "Really? Care to introduce me?"

He crossed his arms over his chest and didn't seem inclined to move from guarding the door—which kept her pretty well trapped in the bathroom. She stared at his expression, judging his sincerity, and couldn't miss the genuine interest in his eyes.

She'd never, ever told anyone about the duo, not even her father. But in a very short span of time she'd come to trust Christian, and knew that just as he'd understood about her array of colorful designer shoes, he'd understand this particular quirk about her, as well.

"Well, there's Angie on the right, who is the angelic side of my conscience," she said, pointing to her right shoulder, even though she knew Christian couldn't see anyone sitting there. "And then there's Desiree on the left, who is the more daring side. Angie keeps me in line and makes sure I'm doing the *right* thing, and Desiree is the one who is constantly trying to tempt me to be more adventurous."

He chuckled. "I think Desiree and I would get along just fine."

Amanda didn't doubt that for a moment, given his own bad-boy reputation. "They've been with me since I was twelve."

His humor fled, replaced by a serious, tender expression. "When your mother died?" he asked.

She was amazed that he'd made that connection, which proved just how much he'd paid attention during their conversation yesterday. "I went through a really tough time after my mother passed away, especially since she was a stay-at-home mom. All of a sudden, I was coming home to an empty house after school until my father got home from work. So, I felt as though I had to make a lot of decisions on my own."

A small, knowing smile curved the corner of his mouth. "And that's where Angie and Desiree come in?"

Nodding, she leaned back against the bathroom counter, suddenly aware of the fact that she was still only wearing a towel. But, it was obvious that Christian wasn't letting her go anywhere until she finished explaining.

"Whenever I had an issue with peer pressure, or something came up with a friend that I didn't know how to handle, Angie was there to try and guide me in the right direction, while Desiree did her best to coax me into trouble. But, in the end, Angie usually won because I didn't want to give my father any reason to be disappointed in me, in any way."

"I think your father is very proud of the woman you've become," he said, as if he knew for certain it was so.

"I think so, too," she said and smiled. "But who knows how I would have ended up without Angie and Desiree's influence."

"You would have ended up just as you are. An incredibly smart and beautiful woman, inside and out." He pushed away from the door and closed the distance between them. Placing his hands on the curve of her waist, he leaned into her, intimately close. "*You're* the one who made all the right decisions and choices throughout the years, Amanda. And if it helps you to believe that you had a bit of assistance along the way, well, there's nothing wrong with that."

She reached up and placed her palm on his cheek, and swallowed past the surge of emotion crowding in her chest. "Thank you," she whispered, wondering if he realized just how much his words meant to her. It was as if he understood how insecure and vulnerable she'd been after her mother's death, and now that she'd finally talked about that time in her life, she suddenly felt lighter. Stronger in both mind and spirit.

It was an awesome, overwhelming feeling, one she wholeheartedly welcomed.

And she owed this man for setting a part of her free and for giving her such a precious gift.

"But you know what?" he said as a seductive, mischievous gleam entered his eyes, changing the mood from serious to playful. "I have to agree with Desiree. You really do need to be more adventurous."

She thought about the shoes he'd asked her to wear, the things they'd done with the tie and scarf that even now made her blush. She'd stepped out of her comfort zone with Christian numerous times, and had loved every minute of it. "Don't you think I've been plenty daring this weekend?"

"Eh," he said, the one word sounding much too doubtful as he lifted her so she was sitting on the vanity and her spread legs bracketed his hips. "Honestly? I think you still need a few more lessons before you're fully qualified as daring."

She lifted a brow and shivered as his hands slipped beneath the hem of her towel and up her bare thighs. "Oh, really?"

"Oh, yeah," he replied before dipping his head and nuzzling his face against her neck.

His palms skimmed over her hips and around to her bottom, causing the knot securing the towel at her breasts to unravel and fall to the sides, baring her naked body and inviting his gaze, his touch, and anything else he wanted to do to her.

"So, what did you have in mind?" she asked breathlessly. A stupid, ridiculous question considering his mouth was already traveling down to her aching breasts.

His hands cupped her bottom and pulled her to the very edge of the counter, until his jean-clad erection pressed insistently against her damp, sensitive flesh. "Ever had slow, hot sex on a bathroom vanity?"

Her stomach muscles clenched in anticipation. "I can't say I have." He flicked one of her nipples with his tongue, and she tangled her fingers into his silky-soft hair, dropped her head back and moaned.

"Well, then, there you go," he said and smiled against the curve of her breast while his hands went to work unfastening his jeans and releasing his shaft. "Another brand new adventure for you to enjoy."

Somewhere in the bathroom cabinet he found a condom and slipped it on. She gasped as the head of his erection glided through her slick, feminine folds, then oh-so-gradually pushed into her, until he was all the way in and filling her completely. With a low, primitive groan, he crushed his mouth to hers and kissed her, as deeply and slowly as he made love to her body. She whimpered as sensations built upon sensations, as the lazy thrust and agonizingly slow retreat of his hips made her desperate to feel the hot length of him driving harder and deeper inside her.

But he didn't give in to her impatience and instead took her on a long, erotic journey that escalated into a sexual inferno between them one last time. When he finally allowed her explosive orgasm to crest, he was right there with her, both of them shuddering with the most exquisite, sublime pleasure she'd ever known.

Christian came to a stop at a red light and glanced at Amanda, who was sitting in the passenger seat of his car. Ever since they'd left his place, she'd been talking nonstop, barely even giving him a chance to respond to anything she had to say. It was just a long stream of inconsequential conversation on her end, and it was making his head spin.

This sort of fidgety behavior was so unlike the poised, in-control Amanda he'd once known, and it had taken him longer than usual to figure out what was wrong. But, once he'd pinpointed where the change in her had begun, the shift from calm and relaxed to anxious and uncertain all made sense to him.

Everything had been fabulous between them after their escapade in the bathroom, and even during breakfast. The shift had come when he'd told her that he needed to take her home so he could get on the road to Boston for Christmas eve with his family. At first, she'd grown quiet, then once they were in his car she'd started talking…and hadn't stopped since.

The light turned green, and he continued down the street toward her place, recognizing her endless chatter for the diversion it was, along with the false brightness in her tone. She was nervous, and he was guessing that she didn't want to deal with a *weekend-after* kind of conversation before they reached her apartment. The kind of discussion that would put an end to their temporary affair, allowing them to go their separate ways without anyone ever knowing what had transpired between them.

The funny thing was, despite promising her that their weekend together would stay just between the two of them, he didn't want this blossoming relationship to end, and he couldn't remember the last time he'd ever felt that way about a woman. It was true that he'd gone into this affair with Amanda with the sole expectation of finally getting her out of his system. But despite those not-so-noble intentions, during the course of their two days together something had changed, and he knew she felt it, too. Beyond the physical pleasure they'd shared, they'd connected on a deeper, more intimate level.

She'd become so much more than just the boss's daughter to him. So much more than a co-worker he'd been attracted to. She'd become a woman he cared for very deeply. A woman who struck an emotional chord in him and made him think about the future, and a series of *what if* questions he'd never contemplated before.

He contemplated them now with Amanda.

Her building came into sight, and he pulled into the circular drive by the front entrance. "I'll walk with you up to your place," he said.

"You don't need to do that," she said, much too cheerfully. "I'll be fine, really. You need to get on your way to Boston."

No, he really didn't. Whatever was between them was far more important. He hesitated, then decided to get it all out there in the open. "Amanda, about this weekend—"

She placed her fingers on his lips, stopping him mid-sentence. She shook her head and managed a smile that was far too fragile. "Please don't say anything, okay?" she pleaded in a voice brimming with what sounded like tears. "I had a great time with you. Thank you for everything."

Okay, the last thing he wanted was her gratitude, and he hated that she was brushing him—and their time together—off. "Amanda—"

This time it was her lips that cut him off, along with a quick, hot kiss that felt way too vulnerable and bittersweet. Finally, she broke the kiss and moved back to her side of the vehicle.

"Merry Christmas, Christian," she said, then bolted out of the car before he could say or do anything to stop her.

He sat there in front of the entrance for a good five minutes, debating whether or not to go up to Amanda's apartment or leave her alone for the time being. After mentally grappling with both scenarios, he finally decided to put the car back into gear and head toward Boston.

Judging by her actions, she wasn't ready to hear anything he had to say, and was obviously under the assumption that she was just another notch on his belt. Without a doubt, he had the reputation to back up those thoughts, but it appeared that his life was about to take a different direction, and she was the reason.

Okay, so she needed more time to calm down and let him explain. Fine, he'd give her that bit of space while he was in Boston. But once he returned, they were going to talk, even if he had to tie her up to force her to listen to what he had to say.

Chapter Six

"So, how's work going, Christian?" one of his older sisters, Kathy, asked as she walked into their parents' living room from the kitchen and handed him a cold bottle of beer. "Last we all heard at Thanksgiving you were still the number-one sales executive and working toward the sales director position."

"I still am." He thanked his sister for the beer and took a drink, watching with a smile as his youngest nieces and nephews chased each other through the house, despite the fact that their mothers had already warned them to quit being so wild and rambunctious. "It should be decided after the holiday."

"Well, you deserve it," his other sister, Diane, said as she set a tray of ham-and-cream-cheese roll-ups on the coffee table for everyone to enjoy. "We all know how hard you've worked toward this promotion."

"To the point that he's become a confirmed bachelor, instead of settling down like the rest of you have," his mother complained from her position on the couch across the room.

Christian rolled his eyes because this was a scenario he relived every time he came home for a visit. His mother's greatest wish was to see all her children happily married with a family of their own. So far, he was the only one who hadn't conformed to her expectations. "Now, Mom…"

"You know it's true," she went on and looked to their father for confirmation, but he wisely remained quiet. "How many times have you told me that you're just too busy furthering your career to settle down?"

"Too many times to count," Kathy offered before Christian could reply, and laughed. "Don't worry, Mom. It'll happen. He just needs to meet the right woman for him, and once he does, I can guarantee he'll change his way of thinking."

A greater truth had never been spoken, Christian thought. He hadn't been looking for Mrs. Right, but she'd happened along anyway, and he wasn't about to let her slip from his life, if he could help it.

He'd been at his parents for a few hours now, and his thoughts were never far from Amanda. In fact, he'd already pulled his cell phone from his pocket five times with the intention of calling her to talk things through, but managed to restrain himself. After the way she'd scrambled from his car earlier, he knew she wasn't ready to hear what he had to say, and he hoped to God that a few days apart might help his cause and make her listen to reason.

"Christian, I'm thinking you must have paid a small fortune to have those presents you brought with you wrapped," Diane teased, pulling his attention away from his troubling thoughts to yet another topic that made him think of Amanda and the time they'd spent together over the weekend.

"I have to agree," Kathy commented from her seat close to the Christmas tree and the gifts piled beneath. "They look like they were professionally decorated."

"Sorry to disappoint the two of you, but they weren't wrapped by a professional, and it didn't cost me anything." Grinning, he reached for one of the delicious stuffed mushrooms his mother always made as a holiday appetizer and popped it into his mouth.

"Well, we all know that *you* didn't wrap them," Diane said, the curiosity in her tone unmistakable. "Wrapping presents is so not your forte."

His younger brother, Brian, who was sitting next to him on the couch and had been quiet up to this point while he chowed down on the appetizers, finally had something to add to the conversation. He slapped Christian on the back in male camaraderie and said, "He's probably dating a gift-wrap clerk over the holidays and that's just one of the perks of their fling."

"She's not a fling," Christian said automatically, then realized too late how defensive he sounded.

Everyone else noticed, though, and the adults in the room went quiet. Now, they were all staring at him with open interest and speculation.

"Whoa, you're really dating a gift-wrap clerk?" Brian asked around the ham roll-up he'd just stuffed into his mouth.

"Since when have you had a serious relationship?" Diane asked in shock.

His mother didn't hesitate to chime in, as well. "And if it's *that* serious, why haven't you told *us* about her?"

He sighed, and tried to explain. "Because it just *recently* became serious."

Brian stared at him incredulously. "Holy shi—"

"Watch your language," his wife, Sarah, said, cutting off her husband before the words were out of his mouth. "The kids can hear you."

"Holy *cow*," Brian said as he slanted Sarah a wry look before glancing back at Christian. "I do believe my brother is finally whipped."

Christian just smiled, knowing that his silence, and the fact that he didn't argue, spoke volumes.

An excited gleam entered his mother's eyes. "So, when do we get to meet this woman?"

He rolled his beer bottle between his palms and

shrugged. "Just as soon as I can convince *her* that it's serious between us."

Brian let out a loud guffaw. "Oh, man, it's so sweet to finally see the invincible love 'em and leave 'em playboy on the other side of the fence."

Despite the truth of his brother's statement, Christian wasn't the least bit amused. "Her name is Amanda, and she's my boss's daughter," he said, just so everyone knew exactly what he was up against.

That earned him a gasp from his sister Diane, whose expression had softened considerably. "Oh, Christian, that can't be good for your upcoming promotion."

That particular concern had crossed his mind, as well, during the drive to Boston, because the possibility did exist that Douglas might not take too kindly to the fact that Christian wanted to pursue his daughter, considering his past indiscretion at the office. But Christian had come to a very important decision, and he shared it with his family.

"When I get back home, I plan to talk to Amanda and try to convince her to give us a chance," he said. "My job is very important to me, and I do care about the promotion, but if push comes to shove and I have to make a choice, I care about Amanda more."

As for her father, somehow, someway, he'd make Douglas Creighton understand just how much Amanda meant to him.

Excitement welled up inside of Amanda as she sur-veyed the floor-to-ceiling rack in her closet displaying all the bright, colorful designer shoes she'd bought over the years. They all looked shiny and brand new, with nary a scratch or scuff to mar the closed-toe shoes or the expensive leather straps on the high heels.

Now that she'd decided to put the shoes to *real* use, it was like having a sweet tooth and being set free in a candy store to gorge on all your favorite treats. But the difficult part was which treat did she indulge in first?

She bit her bottom lip and glanced down at the new outfit she'd bought yesterday at a department store's day-after-Christmas sale. Her father had given everyone an extra day off from work to enjoy the holiday weekend a little longer, and Amanda had spent the day shopping and updating her wardrobe to reflect the new her.

She'd replaced her practical, businesslike suits with ones that were more feminine. She'd added lace to her tops, chosen bolder colors and went a few inches shorter on her skirts. Instead of long, double-breasted jackets, she'd selected a few cropped, fitted ones that showed off her figure, rather than hid her curves.

She'd implemented subtle, sensual changes in her choice of clothing, and today she was wearing a fitted suede jacket in a gorgeous color of azure-blue, a pretty cream-hued camisole beneath and an A-line black skirt that ended a few inches *above* her knee, instead of below. Now, all she needed to do was pick out a pair of shoes to complement the outfit.

After much deliberation, she finally settled on a pair of Manolo Blahnik sling-back heels with colorful, sexy straps that crisscrossed over her foot. She carried them into her bedroom, and with an undeniable burst of exhilaration she slipped them on, then turned to face her reflection in her dressing mirror to finally check out the end results.

So, you're really going to wear those shoes outside of the apartment?

"Yeah, I am." Amanda smiled at Angie, who'd appeared on her right shoulder and was taking in all the new changes in Amanda's appearance. Despite the slight concern creasing her guardian angel's brows, there had been no censure or scandal in her voice. Just an acceptance of the decisions Amanda had made over the past few days. "I'm going to wear those designer shoes to work, and to dinners, and anywhere else I can."

Well, good for you, Desiree piped in and applauded Amanda's new attitude.

"Thank you very much." Amanda gave the cheeky devil a slight bow for her praise. "In fact, all my old, sensible pumps are getting dropped off at Goodwill since I won't be needing them anymore."

Oh, yeah! Desiree punched her first in the air triumphantly, her voice infused with pride. *You go, girl!*

Laughing at Desiree's enthusiastic response, Amanda walked toward her dresser and picked up the scarf that Christian had given her for Christmas. A gift that had so much thought and meaning behind it. She slid the vibrant silk through her fingers, and a huge lump gathered in her throat when she thought of their last moments together, and the paralyzing fear that had gripped her.

When Christian had dropped her off on Sunday and started his goodbye with the dreaded *about this weekend* phrase, she'd been so certain that he was going to try and let her down gently, or remind her that their time together was only a two-night deal. She'd been so afraid of being rejected after the most incredible weekend of her life that she hadn't given him the chance to say anything at all. She didn't want to hear the words that would pierce her heart, and it had been so much easier for her to be the one to walk away first, rather than be devastated by a brush-off.

But now that she'd had a few days alone to think about her behavior, she realized just what a coward she'd been. And how unfair, too. She hadn't given Christian any opportunity to say what was on his mind, and had anticipated the worst—even after he'd been so caring and understanding with her. She'd been very wrong to assume anything, and knew that good or bad, she needed to hear whatever Christian had to say to her.

The old Amanda would have gone to work and pretended nothing had ever happened between them. But this new Amanda, the woman in the mirror who felt so confident and sexy because of Christian's encouragement, was going to face issues head-on and take the kind of risks she'd avoided in the past. Risks like telling Christian how she really felt about him. She hoped that he felt the same. And if he didn't, well, at the very least she'd like to think they could be friends.

Are you going to be okay?

She knew that Angie was concerned about her emotional state after her weekend with Christian, but Amanda truly couldn't have felt more optimistic about her future, regardless of the outcome with Christian. "I'm going to be fine. More than fine," she reassured Angie with a genuine smile. "In fact, there's something I need to tell the two of you."

Desiree and Angie grew somber, as if they both knew what she was going to say.

"You two have been in my life for so long, but it's

time for me to be on my own." Being with Christian had made her realize that she needed to make her own choices, that she no longer needed the emotional crutch of having Desiree and Angie around. She now understood that it was all about her letting them go. Not the other way around.

You're right. Our work is done here, Desiree said, and Amanda could have sworn she saw a glimmer of moisture in the she-devil's eyes.

Yes, you're ready to be on your own, Angie agreed softly, and with pride.

When Amanda glanced back into the mirror, the duo was gone. But, surprisingly, she didn't feel as though anything was ending. Rather, it was the start of a new beginning.

Christian was nervous as hell, and that was saying a lot since he was normally so cool, calm and collected even under the most stressful of situations. But, it wasn't every day that he put his heart, and his job, on the line for a woman.

He'd arrived at work early so he could catch Douglas Creighton before everyone started arriving at the office. But now that he was sitting across from his boss, his stomach was in knots because he couldn't even begin to anticipate the end result of this conversation.

He exhaled a deep breath and jumped right in. "Thanks for seeing me so early. There's something important I'd like to talk to you about."

"Sure," Douglas said easily. "What's on your mind?"

There was no sense in beating around the bush, and he got right to the point. "I want to see your daughter."

The older man frowned, clearly confused. "You see her every day at the office."

Christian shook his head and chuckled, releasing the tension that had been tightening his chest. "Okay, maybe I need to be more specific. I want to *date* your daughter. Exclusively."

This announcement was met with silence and a narrowing of Douglas's gaze. Before the other man could launch himself across the desk and strangle Christian for even suggesting such a thing, he figured he might as well get everything out in the open and really give Creighton a reason to kill him.

"I spent some time with Amanda over the weekend, and I want to continue spending time with her without sneaking around," he said on a rush of breath. "I wanted to be honest with you so you would know my intentions right up front."

Douglas leaned back in his chair and stared at

Christian for what seemed like hours, when in fact only a minute had passed before the older man rubbed a hand along his jaw and finally spoke. "I certainly respect your honesty, but given your past indiscretion here in the office, I can't help but be a bit concerned about Amanda's reputation."

"I understand," Christian said, knowing that Douglas's worries were valid, all things considered. "But I do care for her, and I wouldn't be in here, risking my promotion to be with her if I didn't feel she was worth it."

"Yes, I suppose you are putting that promotion on the line." Douglas studied him again, and Christian wished he knew what the other man was searching for. "You know, Amanda has had trouble in the past with men wanting to date her to get to me. They were more interested in what I could do for them than they were in her."

"No, I didn't know that," Christian said, but realized how this situation must look to Douglas. However, he could only prove his sincerity over the course of time. *If* he walked out of here with Creighton's blessing.

"However, I can honestly say that none of those other men had the guts and integrity that you do, to come to me and risk your job as you have."

"Thank you, sir," Christian said, hoping his candor

counted for something in the end. "I think finding the right woman makes all the difference in the world."

"Ahhh, that they do," Douglas said with a smile. "You do know that behind every great man is an even greater, stronger woman, right?"

Christian grinned. "So my own father has said, numerous times."

"Smart man, and he's passing some good, solid advice on down to his son." Douglas sat forward in his chair again, his gaze direct and all business. "Now, about that promotion. I had every intention of giving it to you. However, after this conversation—"

Christian held up a hand to stop his boss, disappointed, but knowing he could better deal with the loss of the promotion if he didn't actually hear the words out loud. "I completely understand."

Douglas tipped his head and clasped his hands together on his desk. "Do you?"

Christian nodded. "You want to make sure I'm not like all those other guys, and I'm not out to use your daughter for a promotion, or anything else for that matter."

"Actually, I already know you're not like all those other men she's dated." The confidence in Douglas's voice rang true. "You've proved yourself within the company, and again today, right now, that you're a man who's loyal and values honesty. I can't ask for more than that. The sales director position is yours, Christian."

Stunned, it took a few extra seconds for the reality of Douglas's words to sink in, and when they did, Christian stood up and shook his boss's hand. "Thank you," he managed to say, still dazed.

"You're welcome. You've earned it. I was going to wait until after the first of the year to announce the promotion, but I figure there's no better time than the present."

Christian sat back down in his seat, trying to take it all in.

"Back to my daughter," Douglas said, redirecting the conversation to what Christian had originally come into his office for. "I met her for breakfast this morning, and now I know why she looked so sparkly, bright and alive. *You're* the reason."

Sparkly and bright? Christian frowned in confusion over those words. "Excuse me?"

Douglas laughed in amusement. "Ahhh, you obviously haven't seen her yet today, have you?"

"No. I wanted to talk to you first."

Creighton glanced at his wristwatch, noting the time. "Well, she should be in her office by now. And since we're done here, I suggest you don't keep my daughter waiting any longer."

Christian grinned. "Yes, sir," he said and hightailed

it out of there.

✧   ✧   ✧

Riding on a huge high of adrenaline, Christian headed toward Amanda's office, and felt a surge of disappointment when he realized she wasn't inside sitting behind her desk. As he cast a quick glance around, he noticed that the double doors connecting to the private room behind her office were opened. Hearing noises from within, he stepped into the room and quietly closed and locked the doors behind him.

Moving deeper inside, he caught sight of her in the kitchenette making a pot of coffee. Her back was to him, and he waited patiently for her to finish. Finally, she turned back around and started for the doors, then came to an abrupt halt when she saw him standing there.

"Christian!" she said, her eyes wide and startled. "I didn't hear you come in."

He opened his mouth to reply, then snapped it shut again as he took in her outfit. Now he understood what her father had meant by sparkly, bright and alive. That was exactly how Amanda looked to him now. The stunning changes in her showed in her eyes, the way she carried herself and those telltale heels she was wearing on her feet that made her legs look so damn long and sexy. Then there was the scarf that he'd given her that she'd tied loosely around her neck and tucked into the lapels of her jacket. The dazzling colors looked so good on her, and a part of him wondered why she'd worn the scarf when it held so many provocative memories for the two of them.

"Wow," he finally said around the knot in his throat. "You look *amazing*." So much so that he ached to touch her, kiss her and feel her all soft and warm in his arms. They'd only spent a few days apart, and he truly missed everything about her.

"Thank you." She accepted his compliment with a smile and strolled toward him. "I'm glad you're here, because I want to talk to you."

He shook his head. "No, I want to talk to *you,* and this time you're going to listen to me. I even locked the door so you couldn't bolt on me again."

She laughed, but he didn't know what he'd said that she thought was so funny. "That really wasn't necessary."

"Yeah, well, I'm not taking any chances this time." With that said, he took her hand and led her across the room. He was glad when she didn't try and pull away because he was fully prepared to do whatever it took to make her listen to him.

When they reached the couch, he sat down, then pulled her onto his lap. She gasped, surprised by his bold move, but let him have his way and remained sitting on his thighs. A slightly amused smile tugged at her mouth, and he had no idea why she wasn't taking all this more seriously.

He made sure he had her full attention before getting started. "What I have to tell you is very straightforward and simple. When we agreed to get together this past weekend, I never thought it would be anything more than a brief affair. I also never expected that I'd fall so hard for you. But I did."

A slow breath eased out of her, and her gaze softened as she lifted her hand and touched the tips of her fingers tenderly to his jaw. "I did, too," she whispered. "I'm halfway in love with you."

Relief shuddered through him. Oh, God, he felt like the luckiest guy in the world, and he grinned like a fool. "Looks like we'll have to work on that other half, now won't we?"

She laughed huskily. "Don't worry, I have a feeling it won't take much at all for me to fall totally and completely in love with you."

He wrapped an arm around her waist and pulled her closer, so that she was pretty much plastered against his chest. "So, you'll date me?" he asked and placed a soft, teasing kiss on her lips. "You'll be my girlfriend and turn down any guy that shows even a glimmer of interest in asking you out? Because I have a feeling that those sexy shoes of yours are going to attract a whole lot of attention."

She framed his face in her hands, her eyes shining with affection and adoration, and a whole lot of happiness. "The only attention I care about is yours."

"Good answer," he said and kissed her fully and deeply, until they were both breathless and aroused. "I'm so crazy about you, Amanda. I want to be with you. I want you to meet my family. And I really, really want to take your clothes off and make love to you, right here and now."

She shivered at his words, but the desire heating her gaze gave way to a bit of concern. "We need to tell my father about us."

"I already have." A huge grin spread across his face. "He gave me his blessing, and the promotion. I'm now officially the director of sales."

"Congratulations!" she said excitedly. "That's incredible!"

"No, you are." He touched the scarf around her neck and looked into her eyes, needing to know something. "Did you do all this for me? Wear the scarf, and the shoes, and your new outfit?"

She shook her head. "No, I did it for *me*. It was time for a change. Past time, really."

Her answer was exactly what he wanted and needed to hear. "Then you did it for all the right reasons."

She threaded her fingers through the hair at the

nape of his neck. "And I have *you* to thank for making me realize who I really am deep inside."

He placed his hand on her bare knee and slowly skimmed his palm upward, loving the feel of her soft, smooth skin beneath the tips of his fingers. "Ummm, it was my pleasure."

She raised a brow. "I do believe if you continue in that direction, the pleasure is going to be all mine."

"Yours, mine, ours." He shrugged. "It's all the same."

Before she could issue a comeback, he gently, play-fully tumbled her back onto the couch and pushed the hem of her skirt up to her hips. With a purely wicked grin he dipped his head and gave the inside of her thigh a love bite, which he immediately soothed with his tongue.

"Oh, yes," she moaned softly.

A thought occurred to him, and he stopped and lifted his head so he could look up at Amanda. "Uh, are Angie and Desiree here?" Now that he knew about the two, he didn't care to have them as voyeurs every time he made love to Amanda.

She laughed, obviously knowing why he'd asked that particular question. "No. They're gone. It's just you and me and no more interruptions."

"Thank God," Christian said with a laugh, then set about finishing what he'd just started.

ABOUT THE AUTHOR

Janelle Denison is a *USA Today* Bestselling author of over fifty contemporary romance novels. She is a two time recipient of the National Reader's Choice Award, and has also been nominated for the prestigious RITA award. Janelle is a California native who now calls Oregon home. She resides in the Portland area with her husband and daughters, and can't imagine a more beautiful place to live. When not writing, she can be found exploring the great Northwest, from the gorgeous beaches to the amazing waterfalls and lush mountains. To learn more about Janelle and her upcoming releases, you can visit her website at:

www.janelledenison.com

Other places to find Janelle on the internet:
facebook.com/janelledenisonfanpage
twitter.com/janelledenison

Made in the USA
San Bernardino, CA
03 December 2017